D'oro's fragile floating dream of searching endlessly for Bret through a frozen land of ice-crystal trees and glistening snowdrifts began to fade. She felt weightless and giddy with a sensation of falling through empty space.

Bret's lips descended slowly, touching hers lightly, and D'oro could feel his breath faintly against her tongue. Then his mouth became masterful, exploring, questioning. Her pulse pounded at her temples and echoed at the hollow of her throat. Desire such as she had never known in her well-monitored life began to run through her, taking her to a place she had never been before....

Dear Reader,

It is our pleasure to bring you romance novels that go beyond category writing. The settings of **Harlequin American Romance** give a sense of place and culture that is uniquely American, and the characters are warm and believable. The stories are of "today" and have been chosen to give variety within the vast scope of romance fiction.

As an Air Force wife, Ida Hills has spent a lot of time traveling. She has chosen the mother-lode country of California as the setting for this novel, and I know you'll be on the edge of your seat as her book twists and turns toward its exciting conclusion!

From the early days of Harlequin, our primary concern has been to bring you novels of the highest quality. **Harlequin American Romance** is no exception. Enjoy!

Vivian Stephens

Vivian Stephens
Editorial Director
Harlequin American Romance
919 Third Avenue,
New York, N.Y. 10022

Heartbreaker Mine

IDA HILLS

Harlequin Books

TORONTO • NEW YORK • LONDON
AMSTERDAM • PARIS • SYDNEY • HAMBURG
STOCKHOLM • ATHENS • TOKYO • MILAN

In appreciation
for technical help from my son,
the gold miner.

Published December 1983

First printing October 1983

ISBN 0-373-16034-8

Printed in Canada

Chapter One

Ann Baxter rested the horse's hoof against her leg and ran a reassuring hand down his gleaming black side. With experienced fingers she examined the stone bruise on his foot.

"Damn," she exploded when the horse shied at her touch. "Easy, Megatite. Sorry, old boy," she soothed.

"Megatite! What kind of a name is that for a quarter horse?" her jockey had once asked scornfully. He was more impressed when she explained that in the California gold country megatite was the magnetic black sand in which precious metals were found. But there would be no gold or silver for Megatite that week. Ann would have to scratch him from the race, and she was undecided whether to enter a substitute or pass the Fresno meet. In more than twenty years of breeding quarter horses, Ann couldn't recall not having had an entry in the Fresno races.

She was still mulling over the problem when she heard the sound of Bret Johnson's pickup entering the front drive. Pleasure showed in her intelligent brown eyes as she tied the horse's halter rope to a fence post and hurried to meet her guest. Ann ran her sun-browned competent hands down her slim hips to wipe any dust on her jeans. They were not designer jeans and were faded and well washed. Their snug, comfortable fit announced that they had been her regular work clothes since long before blue jeans became stylish. As she walked across the corral she ran her fingers through her windblown short brown hair. Ann's natural wave caused her hair to fall easily into place, revealing a thin dramatic streak of white at her left temple. She was a small woman with quick, graceful movements that made her age indeterminable.

Bret's work-scarred Dodge pickup was already parked at the gate. He opened the door and stepped out in one fluid motion, causing a painful stirring in Ann's memory that she often felt when she watched him move. He was a tall man, lean and hard with broad shoulders. He had the build of a gold miner, but there was an elegance about the way he wore his expensive, well-tailored clothes that marked him as something more. He flashed her a quick, easy smile, but did not go to meet her. Instead he turned and went back to the Volkswagen that had been following him. Ann felt sure that the driver would be the new laboratory technician Bret had been expecting from Mexico.

A large black Belgian sheep dog bounded from the pickup at Bret's heels. He was an aloof, aristocratic animal, beautifully proportioned with a long regal nose. His silky black coat gave evidence of careful grooming. The dog allowed nothing to interfere with his tested friendships. He went bounding up to greet Ann to receive his expected pat. "Good boy, Thor."

Looking up, Ann Baxter was surprised to see Bret helping a tall blond woman from the VW. She was strikingly pretty with a fresh natural charm—a marked contrast to Bret's recent companions. There was something familiar about the blonde that tugged at her memory, though she was certain she had never met her.

"Annie—Miss Baxter—this is D'oro Griegos, my new laboratory technician from Mexico. Or did you say you have decided the name is Gregg, since you're here?" Bret asked, turning cold suspicious eyes toward the newcomer.

Ann was glad that the antagonism that sparked between Bret and the woman covered her own shock at hearing the name. Gregg was a fairly common name. Jim's daughter couldn't be that old...could she? Somewhere from her subconscious came the very prompt reply that it had been twenty years.

Quickly she extended her hand. "Call me Annie—everyone does. It confirms my status as a local character." She smiled up into the taller woman's startling silver-gray eyes and shock waves went through her. She really was seeing ghosts that day.

"I'm glad to meet you," D'oro responded warmly. She hesitated, then turned impishly to Bret. "Since I'm back in California, I guess Gregg will do, but don't you dare translate the D'oro to Goldie."

Annie chuckled and saw the trace of a smile play across Bret's rugged face before it froze into impassiveness again. She could understand Bret's reaction. Like most miners, he considered lab work to be strictly a man's job. It hadn't occurred to him, or to her, either, that the metallurgist from the Rodriguez Laboratory in Zacatecas, Mexico, might be a woman, and a young, attractive American at that. The name D'oro on the application was one anyone might acquire in a Mexican mining town. She knew that Bret did not believe that the young woman had the complex technical skill to adapt the Rodriguez Process to his ore, making possible the construction of a silver mill in Mariposa.

Bret had been doing very well financially since he made the new strike at the Heartbreaker Mine— as he had been so sure he would when he convinced Annie to sell it to him. But his dreams, his ambition, went beyond that. A local mill would bring new life to the mines and the people of the whole gold-producing area they lovingly called the Mother Lode. Looking at him, Annie was sure that those dreams vanished for Bret the moment he learned that the laboratory technician he was expecting was the pretty blond woman looking at him with defiant eyes. Annie knew that if her painful intuition was right and D'oro Gregg was Jim's daughter—with his keen intelligence, determination, and understanding of silver mining— Bret Johnson would be in for a surprise: However, it wouldn't hurt him to eat a little humble pie.

"We didn't expect you until tomorrow," Annie told D'oro, then turning to Bret she said, "Bring in her things." The older woman led the way into the house as D'oro walked behind with Bret.

"So Annie was expecting your laboratory assistant from Mexico to stay at the ranch. What was all that macho jazz back at the mine about my sharing the trailer with you and Thor?" D'oro demanded when Annie was out of earshot.

"Just wanted to discover all the talents of my new assistant," he said in an insinuating tone that brought a flush of color to highlight D'oro's fine cheekbones and ignited sparks in her steel-gray eyes.

"I don't recall your advertisement in the mining journal listing any duties other than laboratory technician," she snapped.

"Thor was hoping you could cook. He loves Mexican food."

"I'll have to remember to invite him to dinner."

Bret laughed with a rich, deep, natural sound, making his rugged face take on the same easy charm that he had greeted her with when she arrived at the mine—before he learned that D'oro was the laboratory assistant whose application he had accepted. He seemed equally put out that she was not male and that she was not Mexican—at least not by birth.

Bret removed her suitcases from the VW and carried them as if they were weightless compared to the ore he worked with.

D'oro felt an odd reaction to the thick-walled

adobe ranch house to which he led her. It looked like the haciendas built by the early Californians from Mexico, but she was sure it wasn't that old. The shade of the broad portico looked inviting after the heat of the late September day. The handsome hand-carved oak door stood open, and as D'oro looked at the skillful workmanship she had the strangest feeling that she might almost be entering her own home in Zacatecas.

D'oro was surprised to find that Annie's house was decorated in Spanish colonial style, with red tile floors and whitewashed walls accented by hand-woven Mexican drapes and artifacts of hammered silver and wrought iron.

"Put D'oro's things in the guest room," Annie directed from the kitchen.

"Already you've become a special guest. The lab man was to have stayed in the bunkhouse," muttered Bret, leading her into a spacious bedroom furnished with heavy hand-carved mission furniture. French doors opened onto the patio around which the house was built.

"What a beautiful house," exclaimed D'oro when Annie joined them.

"Thank you. My father had it copied from the early California haciendas when he made the first strike at the Silver Queen."

D'oro was completely charmed by the house, but its similarity to her own home in Zacatecas gave her an eerie feeling, a sensation of having walked through a mirror or a space warp.

"Thor has accepted my invitation to dinner. You'll stay too, won't you?" Annie asked Bret.

"You know who's the boss," he answered lightly.

"Can I help?" offered D'oro.

"No, thanks. I'm used to a one-woman kitchen. Why don't you let Bret show you around the place while I see what I can rustle up."

They crossed the polished red tile floor of the long living room with its open-beam ceiling. Even before Bret opened the French doors at the back, D'oro could visualize the patio that would be there. Only the plants in the big red clay containers were different. In Zacatecas's hot dry climate the plants were succulents and cactus, brightened by colorful dahlias. In California's more friendly climate the flowers were a riot of fall color. D'oro wondered if her father had been familiar with Annie's house when he designed their home.

Beyond the patio the similarity ended. A tall white gate with the letters S/S above it led to a large corral. Bret stopped at the edge of the patio for D'oro to enjoy the picture of neat white-washed fences surrounded by autumn-brown grass against a backdrop of rugged pine-covered mountains.

"Bret, I left Megatite tied in the corral. Would you put him in his stall?" called Annie's rich, husky voice through the open kitchen window.

"Be glad to," he called back as he motioned to D'oro to walk with him.

"Is the S/S a cattle ranch?" D'oro asked.

"No. Annie raises quarter horses."

"What is a quarter horse?"

"A quarter horse is the cowboy's own horse, bred for quick starts and bursts of speed for distances up to a quarter of a mile. They are more compact and muscular than the Thoroughbreds that are part of their ancestry. This gives them greater endurance under the saddle."

Bret did not go directly to the corral where the black horse was tied, but circled the white rail fence to a grove of cottonwoods through which a crystal-clear stream tumbled over a rocky bed.

"There are some nice trout in the deeper pools," he told D'oro. The cool shade and the gurgling of the stream seemed to relax the tension between them, and D'oro felt an easy amiability toward the man she was to work for by the time they left the cottonwood grove and turned toward the large red barn at the far end of the corral.

Bret stopped beside the black horse and gave him an affectionate pat. "How's the foot, old boy?" He loosened the halter and led the horse toward the barn, watching his slight limp. "No race for you this weekend," he continued as if the horse understood every word. Several other carefully groomed horses stretched out their noses for a pat as Bret passed. He seemed as fond of horses as he was of Thor, who had stayed in the kitchen to supervise the preparation of dinner.

"If these animals are bred for bursts of speed, do you race them?" D'oro asked.

"Oh, yes. There are quarter horse events at most western racing meets. Annie has had a number of track favorites."

A large silver-white stallion at the far end of the

barn began whinnying and pawing the dirt with one front hoof.

"Miss me, old boy?" Bret asked as the horse nuzzled his shoulder.

"Is he yours?"

"Yes. I have a weakness for anything silver. So did Annie's father. That's why he named the ranch Sterling Silver."

"So that's why the brand is S/S, the hallmark for sterling. And your horse is named Silver?" she guessed.

He nodded, grinning in a way that made him appear almost boyish, though he must have been about thirty.

"I hope you don't go riding over the hills, shouting 'Hi-ho, Silver.'"

"At least not where anyone can hear me," he countered as they turned toward the house. "I usually ride Saturday mornings—care to join me?"

"Sounds great," D'oro agreed as Annie summoned them to dinner.

Through the kitchen window Annie watched the easy, graceful movements of the vibrant blond woman with mixed emotions. She had recovered from the initial shock of meeting the living ghost from her own youth. Even before she heard the name she had known that D'oro was Jim's daughter. She looked as much like him as a very feminine woman could look like a man. She had the same classic features, fine bone structure, lithe, slender build, and quick, competent movements. Without the other similarities Annie would have known the eyes, shining silver-gray mirrors of inner depth and sincerity. How many lifetimes had it been since she had looked into Jim's eyes and seen them reflect her own pain and despair? She closed her eyes tightly as if to block out the memory. Why was the woman there? Had Jim sent her? She opened them again as the sound of Bret's rich masculine voice brought her back to the present. There was a quality to his voice that reminded her of Jim. Perhaps that was why she had listened to his entreaties to sell him the Heartbreaker Mine. What sort of Pandora's box had she reopened?

Ann watched as Bret opened the door and the young woman turned to smile up at him. As she did the sun glinted off her long blond hair, the hair that seemed to be D'oro's only inheritance from Sally. How Annie had envied, yet hated that blond hair. She recalled the final crushing blow when Annie learned that Sally was to have Jim's child, and she knew she had lost him forever. Annie took a deep breath, squared her shoulders, and set her chin at the defiant angle that after twenty years had become an instinctive part of her. She picked up a plate of hot biscuits and followed her guests into the dining room.

The room was as handsome as the rest of the house D'oro had seen. It was furnished with mission oak combined with wrought iron. The subdued effect of the furnishings was brightened by a beautiful gleaming silver service on the sideboard that D'oro recognized as Taxco Mexican silver.

The dinner was definitely planned to please a

hungry man—thick T-bone steaks, hot biscuits, mashed potatoes and gravy, and fresh corn on the cob that was so sweet, it must have been picked from nearby fields that day. A rich red Cabernet with a delightful fruity aroma accompanied the dinner.

The conversation was sparkling and witty, touching on a wide range of topics. The one thing that was not mentioned was the mine or the silver recovery process for which D'oro had been hired to work. D'oro acknowledged it could be a reluctance to discuss business during dinner, but she felt it was more than that. While Bret and Annie exchanged anecdotes about the summer tourists from eastern cities who came to Mariposa bent on rediscovering the old mining lore, she studied the man sitting across the table from her. His thick black hair was well cut to follow the contour of his classic head. His eyes, startlingly blue in his sun-bronzed face, crinkled at the corners with amusement. There was a magnetic charm about him as he divided his attention equally between the two women. Since they had arrived at the ranch he had treated her as if she were a houseguest, showing her the land and the stables and entertaining her at dinner. Beneath the charm D'oro felt there was a complete dismissal of her as a serious contributing employee of the Heartbreaker Mine. Why didn't he just say so? She had seen enough of the polite flirtatious games men played with women in Mexico while keeping them firmly in their place. D'oro had hoped to leave that macho attitude behind when she crossed the border.

"What is Zacatecas like?" Annie asked.

The question was so close to D'oro's thoughts that it took her a moment to compose the expected answer. She described the charming colonial town with its pink sandstone buildings contrasting with dun-colored hills. She mentioned the twin-towered cathedral with its ornately carved facade.

"How did you get the name D'oro? Isn't it a bit unusual, even in Mexico?" Annie prompted.

"Our housekeeper, Maria, Juan Rodriguez's sister, gave me the name. Of course, like most children raised in Mexico, I have a long list of Christian names bestowed at baptism, confirmation, and so on." D'oro could see no reason to mention that the name on her birth certificate was Sally, her mother's name. No one had called her that since her beautiful spoiled mother had left them when D'oro was five. "Maria raised me along with her own brood. She insisted I was D'oro, her golden one."

"Then you've known Juan Rodriguez for a long time?" D'oro suspected Annie asked the question more for Bret's information than her own.

"I've tagged around after *Tio* Juan for as long as I can remember. He used to think aloud as if talking to me about his problems when he was developing his formula. Of course, I didn't understand, but my father and I were the only ones at the mine who spoke English, and Juan does all of his research in English. He studied metallurgy at Colorado School of Mines. I've worked in the laboratory since I was old enough to wash test tubes. He promoted me to more scientific tasks during the summers when I was home from boarding school and university.''

"I'm surprised Rodriguez and the company he works for allowed you to bring his formula out of the country, to share it with a potential competitor. Or perhaps he didn't consider what you knew of the process to be a threat?''

Bret's change of mood and the anger that turned his eyes a cold glinting blue caught D'oro by surprise. "Juan doesn't believe a scientific discovery should belong to one man or one company to be hoarded away for their exclusive profit,'' she snapped, her anger rising to meet her challenger.

"Did Juan Rodriguez know about your taking this job?'' Annie cut in.

"Yes. I showed him the advertisement. He was very supportive. Maria was angry at him for encouraging me.''

"Did your . . .'' Annie began, then let the question trail off. She began again. "Did you go to the university in Mexico City?''

D'oro felt it was not the question Annie had started to ask. "No. In Guadalajara. Dad thought that was more my speed after such a conservative remote town as Zacatecas and the good sisters at boarding school.'' The mischievous twinkle in D'oro's snapping gray eyes suggested she had not been the sisters' model student. "It was easier for me to get home for holidays from Guadalajara.''

Bret relaxed and returned to his role of charming dinner companion. D'oro wasn't sure which of his moods upset her most. After dinner they took their coffee to the family room, its comfortable leather chairs and large native stone fireplace continuing the strange duplication of D'oro's home. There was a similarity too between the tall, lean, broad-shouldered man who occupied the big leather armchair and her father, in spite of the difference in their ages. D'oro dismissed the idea as part of the mystifying illusion. They weren't really alike, she told herself sternly. Her father was always completely fair and willing to give each person a chance to prove what he could do.

Again it was Annie who directed the conversation by asking Bret, "How's the new vein developing?"

"It's broadening out as it goes upward. It's proving to be even richer than I had anticipated. Speaking of the mine, it's after hours for this hard-working man." He rose and crossed the room to where Annie was sitting and kissed her affectionately on the cheek. "Dinner was great as always."

His eyes roved speculatively over D'oro's smooth skin and soft mouth. She braced herself for a similar farewell. Immediately she decided she must have been mistaken; his jaw tensed and his tone was completely that of her employer. "I'll see you at the lab at ten. You may as well sleep in, as you've had a long trip."

D'oro started to protest, but the look in his eyes stopped her. He had made it all too obvious it didn't much matter when she got there.

When Annie returned from seeing Bret out, she said in a brusque, friendly way, "If it's any consolation, I think you can do the job for us."

"Thanks for the vote of confidence. Do you have a financial interest in the Heartbreaker?"

"Not anymore. Bret insisted on complete control when he persuaded me to sell it to him, but if you can perfect the process, and Bret sets up a mill, I might reopen the Silver Queen...or sell it." There was a long pause before she added, "It adjoins the Heartbreaker."

Just what had she gotten herself into? D'oro wondered as she lay engulfed in the softness of the big old mission bed so like the one in her room at home. The advertisement in the mining journal had sounded so simple. "Wanted—metallurgist familiar with the Rodriguez Process of silver recovery." She had expected a routine laboratory job with a humdrum computerized American company, not these two dynamic, puzzling people and the strange undercurrents of time and place.

In the other wing of the hacienda Annie tossed restlessly in the big bed that one of the Mexican artisans had hand carved for her father. He had been a big man in every way, and by modern standards the bed was easily king size. She thought of D'oro in her guest room, and of the man she resembled in so many ways—Jim Gregg. Even the name made her ache with longing as she recalled her dream of one day sharing that bed with him. She wouldn't have believed the pain could still be so sharp, the memories so fresh after all those years.

It had not been Jim, but Clay Nalton who had brought her as a bride to the bed. Clay, who knew every move, every caress to bring her passion to inescapable ferment. She could almost feel his thick sensuous lips on hers, teaching, coaxing her inexperienced mouth to respond to his—lips that could enflame every sensitive part of her body. With equal skill his hands had caressed, teased, excited.

It had been easy enough to confuse the first fire of unknown passion with love. In the first months of their marriage she had succeeded in convincing herself that she was ecstatically happy, but she was too honest not to face the contradiction between his nighttime performance and his daytime behavior. She could not long ignore the fact that Clay Nalton was cruel, selfish, and greedy in his dealings with her and everyone else with whom he came in contact. Annie learned all too soon that it was dangerous to cross him. She knew well the brutal strength of the man as he possessed her—willingly or not it made no difference. As the relationship grew worse between them and Clay's jealousy of Jim increased, he took perverse delight in his ability to arouse her desire for him.

After all the years, Annie could still feel the turmoil of loathing and passion within her that had embroiled them all in the final tragedy. She buried her face in the soft down pillow and wept, an admission of vulnerability she had not allowed herself for a very long time.

Chapter Two

After almost as hearty a breakfast as Maria had insisted she eat when she was growing up, D'oro drove to the mine. It was a pleasant drive. The valley where Annie's ranch was located was dotted with groves of willow and cottonwood. The main highway wound through rugged pine-clad mountains, a welcome change from central Mexico's sere, almost lunar landscape. D'oro wondered idly why her father had left such a place to live in Mexico.

She smiled when she came to the hand-lettered sign, HEARTBREAKER MINE, that marked the turnoff. She knew all too well what an appropriate name that was for a silver mine. Her life had been completely enmeshed in the struggle for that precious pale metal. She wondered if the mine dated back to the '49 Gold Rush, when such picturesque names were popular.

D'oro parked in the shade of a clump of pine trees at the edge of the clearing instead of following the road to its end beside Bret's mobile home. That way the car would be cooler when she was ready to leave, she told herself. She would not admit that Bret's suggestion when she arrived that she might share his trailer with him had anything to do with her choice of parking place.

When she started down the path through the pines to the laboratory, Thor came to greet her like an old friend, waving his elegantly plumed tail and nudging her hand with his aristocratic nose. In spite of his friendliness D'oro knew she would not want to attempt to approach the mine if she did not have Thor's stamp of approval.

In the bright morning sunlight the mine was as much of a surprise as it had been the previous evening. The silver mines of Zacatecas that had formed the backdrop to her childhood were huge old tunnels, some almost two hundred years old, surrounded by clay-covered slag heaps. Bret's mine was neat, compact, and modern. The area was dominated by a tall slender scaffolding topped by two large pulleys. An ore bucket with wheels attached to the bottom clung to the tracks running up the face of the whitewashed framework. Below the scaffold stood an ore car so small, it might have been used for a children's ride at an amusement park. Heavy steel cables came from a large spool in the hoist house, stretched to the pulleys at the top of the tower, then ran down into the mine. The entrance to the mine looked like an old-fashioned root cellar with large double doors that could be closed and locked.

Having satisfied the requirements of hospitality, Thor had gone to lie in front of the entrance to the mine, where his nose was as close as possible to the cable running down the shaft, and to a red bandanna tied to the cable.

D'oro was glad that Bret had given her a key to the laboratory the previous evening, when he reluctantly accepted the fact that he had no choice but to see what she could do. The laboratory was attached to the hoist house. Its flasks, burners, scales, jars of chemicals, and other equipment for mineral analysis were as neatly organized as the rest of the mine layout. On one side of the room sat several buckets of crushed ore showing gleaming white quartz studded with sparkling flecks and dull blackish-gray dust. She welcomed the opportunity to become familiar with her workroom in her own way at her own pace while Bret was working elsewhere. Looking around the laboratory, it was obvious that Bret was a man who liked everything in its place. Perhaps that was part of the trouble between them. He kept trying to put her in her place, and there was no place where D'oro Gregg belonged. She had always been on the fringe, never quite a part of the Mexican culture in which she was raised. Even though she had returned to what should have been home, the feeling persisted of being on the outside looking in. She shrugged expressively and set to work.

By ten o'clock she had spent an hour checking equipment and supplies. Through the window she saw Thor come alive with excitement and anticipation. He pranced majestically without taking his eyes off the red bandanna, which had begun to bob up and down. In a few minutes Bret's miner's hat appeared above the ladder leading from the shaft.

D'oro studied the man with growing interest. He wore snug-fitting jeans tucked into the tops of high laced boots. A blue plaid wool shirt strained across his broad chest as he moved his shoulders to climb the last few feet up the ladder. The blue of the shirt brought out the brilliant blue of his eyes. The streak of a dirty handprint down one cheek emphasized the rugged handsomeness of his features. There was an elemental strength and independence about the man emerging from the mine that she found totally masculine and exciting. Watching him made her pulse quicken. But that was the part of the man that totally rejected her intrusion into his plans.

Bret paused to pat the eager dog and then walked briskly to the laboratory door with Thor bounding at his heels. He paused, listening for something. Suddenly D'oro heard a low underground rumble, and the building shuddered slightly.

"One," counted Bret. The rumble was repeated and he counted, "Two," then "Three" until there had been ten of the muffled explosions. "All came and all were good," he announced more to himself than to D'oro. Noting the questioning look she gave him, he asked, "Haven't you heard dynamite blasts before?"

Was he testing her again? she wondered. "No. The mines are too remote and the tunnels too deep in the old silver mines at Zacatecas to feel or hear the blasts."

"I usually do my blasting the last thing in the evening, so the fumes are cleared out and the tunnels are ready to work in the morning, but it was late when Thor and I got home last night. I decided to blast early this morning and help you get checked out in the laboratory while the dust and fumes clear.''

D'oro could see a cloud of dust and smoke rising from the mine shaft, and the acrid smell of sulfur began to reach her nostrils.

"How deep is the shaft?" she asked.

"About two hundred feet. Ever been down in a silver mine?"

"Not a working mine. They take tourists down in one of the mines at Zacatecas that is no longer operating. I've been in it several times. Mexican miners are very superstitious that a woman in a mine will cause the vein to pinch out, so I've never been in Dad's mine."

"Your father owns one of the Zacatecas silver mines?" Bret asked dubiously.

"No. He's foreman of the Plata Nueva Mine. We always speak of it as his mine."

"That's where Rodriguez built his mill, isn't it?" he asked, idly tossing a piece of gleaming quartz in his hand as he spoke.

"Yes. How did you learn so much about his work?"

"I worked with his former instructor at Colorado School of Mines. He told me about it, but he didn't know the complete process."

"Have you done any work with aqua regia?" she asked, her fascination with the subject bringing a sparkle to her eyes and animation to her voice.

"The ancient royal water made with nitric and hydrochloric acid that dissolves gold and platinum?" he quoted in a mocking voice that made it clear he thought the idea was a myth.

"Suspends in liquid form would be more accurate than dissolves, since the minerals can be precipitated out again in pure form," she corrected.

"But aqua regia won't extract silver," he objected, dropping the piece of ore in his hand back into the bucket with finality.

"When the Rodriguez formula is used to balance the sulfur content of silver, it will. Do you have nitric and hydrochloric acids?" She turned to look at the cupboard where volatile chemicals were stored.

"Small quantities. They are quite rigidly controlled. We can get larger quantities of the acids from the mining outfitter at Dry Gulch." The look of speculative friendliness in his eyes and the banter in his voice had been replaced by a brusque businesslike acceptance.

D'oro was reminded of how many times Maria had warned her, "A man can't think of you as *bella señorita* and a lady metallurgist at the same time. It is foolishness that Juan has taught you," and she would shrug her ample shoulders expressively. Too bad, D'oro thought. Bret Johnson was a very attractive man when he wanted to be. He was taller than most of her friends in Mexico, giving her the unaccustomed sensation of having to look up to a man when she talked to him. As she paused to study the expression in his startling blue eyes and watch him run his fingers through his casually styled dark hair, she thought that Bret did not look like anyone she had ever seen around a mine before.

"Can I go down in your mine, or are you superstitious, too?"

"I don't suppose another woman would change the vein much. Annie insisted we inspect the mine together before I bought it. It hadn't been worked in over twenty years—closed down when the accident closed the Silver Queen." He glanced at the pad of notes in her hand. "I see you've been busy this morning. Finding everything you need?"

"I've just been looking over the assay and spectrograph reports of the ore. I'll need a pure sample of each mineral in the ore to check how it reacts with the chemicals in the process." As he came closer to look over her shoulder at the reports, D'oro felt acutely aware of his nearness. Her hand holding the report seemed a trifle unsteady.

"I have specimens of free gold and silver in the bottles, and there are plenty of pieces of pure quartz that contain the vein. We can get samples of pure copper, lead, and iron pyrites in Mariposa. We may have to wait until next week when I go to the mine outfitter in Dry Gulch to get the less common minerals and chemicals. Some of the more colorful of the forty-nine ghost towns are up that way. You might enjoy seeing them."

"I'd like that. Are you a native of the gold country?"

"No. The summer I graduated from Mines, I was prospecting the old gold rush country, Death

Valley, and the old forty-nine route. One rainy afternoon I stopped at the Mariposa Historic Museum. I stayed until closing time, looking at the exhibits and examining the specimens of ore donated by the families of early-day miners. You'll have to see them when you're in town. The old safe contains a fortune in gold in every form—nuggets, dust, leaf-crystals, and studded quartz. However, it wasn't the gold that held the most fascination for me. It was a piece of pure white quartz patterned with chunks of gleaming silver. It was from the Silver Queen mine. Annie had donated it to the museum.'' He paused and scowled as if trying to remember something important that nagged at his memory.

"So you got in touch with Annie?''

"Not right away. I located the Silver Queen on my mining map and went out to see it, but it was badly damaged during the cave-in. A short distance away I found the Heartbreaker Mine, which had been closed down intact after the accident. Since I was named for Bret Harte, this mine seemed to be a personal challenge. I felt it was what I had been looking for. Annie was reluctant to sell. I understand she had turned down all previous offers to buy it or the Silver Queen.''

D'oro could imagine how persuasive Bret could be with a woman when he set his mind on something he wanted.

"Where is the Silver Queen?''

"On the back side of this hill. The line between the two claims is just beyond where my pickup is parked.''

"Did you say an accident closed the Silver Queen?"

"Yes. There was a cave-in. The main shaft is pretty well blocked."

"Was anyone hurt?"

"I think Annie's husband was killed in the cave-in. No one will talk much about it."

"Her husband?" repeated D'oro, surprised. "I had the impression her father might have been involved in a tragedy at the Silver Queen."

"No. Her father was killed in an auto accident a year or so before the mine disaster."

"Annie spoke of others interested in a local mill to extract silver. Does she have partners in the Silver Queen?" The word *partners* echoed forbiddingly in D'oro's mind. It was a word that had been part of whispered conversations she had overheard during her childhood that always ended abruptly when the speakers became aware of her presence.

"No partners that I know of. The others she spoke of must have been the families around Mariposa who own old silver or gold mines of lower grade ore who might be able to work them or lease them if I can get a mill in operation using the Rodriguez Process."

"Why haven't they been reopened with gold and silver in such demand?"

"The old California mills were closed and abandoned years ago. The only gold being recovered here is a little scattered free gold being dredged from the streams. The nearest mill to process ore from hard rock mines is in Arizona, and the quality of most of the ore remaining isn't high enough to pay transportation for such a long haul."

"I can't take my gold pan and go find my fortune in the streams after work?" D'oro asked with mock disappointment.

"Not likely. But my chances aren't much better of bringing up from the mine one of those gleaming crystals frosted with pure gold or silver, like the specimens in the museum. The Glory Holes are gone. What gold and silver remains can only be recovered by a lot of hard work and an efficient milling process. Annie shares my dream of what a local mill could mean to the town—to the whole Mother Lode area."

The enthusiasm with which Bret talked of his hopes for the project faded abruptly. For several seconds he stared at the gleaming piece of quartz studded with silver he had picked out of the bucket and been tossing in his hand, then with a doubtful look cast at D'oro he turned and strode out of the lab.

It would always come down to that—his doubt of her ability to do her part of the job, she thought bitterly. "Men!" she flung wordlessly at his retreating back. She looked again at the assay report she was holding in her hand, reading half an ounce of gold, twenty ounces of silver per ton. She knew it was a good commercial grade of ore if an economical recovery method could be worked out. She began listing each mineral mentioned in the spectrograph in preparation for the long, slow process of testing each one of them individually for their reaction to the suspension solution.

By the time she had finished her morning's work and eaten the sandwich she had brought from Annie's, Thor was back watching the bandanna tied to the cable in the mine shaft. She assumed that meant Bret was again working underground, and once more the thought of him made her pulse quicken.

D'oro heard the whir of machinery starting up and the meshing of gears in the hoist house. Looking out the window, she saw the cable Thor had been watching slide smoothly toward its spool. Soon the ore bucket appeared piled high with lumps of red clay not quite hiding the chunks of sparkling white quartz. The bucket climbed the tracks to the top of its scaffold and dumped its contents into the small ore car below with a thunder of falling rock. The car ran to the end of a trestle, tipped automatically, and dumped its contents on a pile of similar material; then it righted itself and returned to its position under the scaffold while the ore bucket dropped back down the shaft.

D'oro watched the process in amazement. It reminded her of the miniature train layout Juan bought for Maria's boys one Christmas, and then spent the whole day playing with it himself. The mines at Zacatecas used very little automation because of the abundance of inexpensive manpower. She knew the system she had just watched would require the work of a very clever mining engineer, one who could easily design and build a recovery mill if she produced a successful extraction formula.

The dumping process was repeated about every half hour, and it required mental discipline for D'oro to concentrate on her work rather than to watch it. When she locked up the laboratory at five o'clock, D'oro lingered a few minutes to see if Bret would be quitting then. As she waited the ore bucket and car went through their dumping routine. When the bucket returned down the mine, the measured movement of the red bandanna indicated another load was being shoveled in. She was about as smart as Thor, she told herself, laughing. She could already tell the difference in the motion when the car was being loaded and when the man was climbing up the ladder beside the cable. She went over and gave the dog a good night pat. He solemnly accompanied her to her car, then trotted proudly back to his post beside the red marker.

D'oro felt disappointed at not seeing Bret again, but it might be just as well, she thought ruefully, remembering the way their encounters always ended in an impasse.

Annie was not in the house when D'oro returned to the ranch. Instead she found a middle-aged Mexican woman putting away cleaning equipment in the broom closet.

"You must be Mr. Bret's new helper. I'm Lupe," the woman said in a deep melodious voice as her dark eyes studied D'oro with interest.

"Yes, I'm D'oro. I'm glad to meet you, Lupe."

"Miss Annie had to go into town. She'll be back for dinner. She said you should make yourself at home."

"Thank you, Lupe." D'oro headed for the back door to have another look at Annie's beautiful horses. None of the handsome animals showed any signs of friendship when she passed their stalls as they had to Bret the previous evening. She paused in front of the brown-and-white spotted horse, which reminded her of the pony her father had given her when she was ten, but the horse ignored her. When she came to the far end of the barn, Bret's big silver stallion seemed particularly indifferent to her presence. Just like his master, she thought. Midway back on the opposite side D'oro stopped abruptly in front of the most beautiful horse she had ever seen. He was a palomino the rich soft color of creamed honey with a mane and tail like silky pampas grass. The horse lifted his proud head and studied her carefully, then extended his nose to be patted. D'oro ran her hand over his soft smooth nose and down his gracefully arched neck, muttering words of admiration.

"Looks like you two are a pretty good match," said a masculine voice with a definite Texas twang.

Surprised, D'oro whirled around to face a small man with leathery skin and twinkling pale blue eyes framed by wisps of gray hair protruding under the rolled brim of a dust-colored ten-gallon hat. If his legs had been less bowed, he might have been as tall as she was, yet with the hat they came out about even.

"Howdy! I'm Rattlesnake Jones, Annie's top wrangler."

"I'm glad to meet you, Mr. Jones." She held out her hand.

The hand that met hers was gnarled and twisted from numerous poorly set breaks, but the grip was so firm, it was a thing to endure. "I'm called Rattlesnake. Beats bein' just plain Johnny Jones."

"Rattlesnake it is, and I'm called D'oro." She smiled. She instantly liked the small cowboy who played his part as if he were in an old western. She thought how different the scene would have been between a senorita and a gaucho in the culture in which she was raised. There would be many such differences there in the place her parents had once called home. Nothing was quite as she had imagined when she had jumped at the chance to go to Mariposa, when she had felt as if the advertisement were somehow meant especially for her.

The palomino nudged D'oro's shoulder, bringing her thoughts back to the reality of the cowboy and the horse.

"I think he's invitin' you, or maybe challengin' you, to a get-acquainted ride," said Rattlesnake.

"May I?" asked D'oro, eager as a child.

"Sure, but it'll have to be just a couple of turns around the corral. I gotta get into town 'fore the feedstore closes," he answered. "Bonanza, meet Miss D'oro." He introduced them solemnly as he took a bridle from a peg beside the stall and slipped it over the horse's handsome head. From the tack room he brought a western saddle that looked almost as big as he was. He slung it on the horse's back in one easy motion and as quickly had it cinched down and ready to go.

"You gotta remember he starts quick, turns quick, and stops quick," he cautioned her as he led the horse out into the corral and held it for her to mount. As soon as he handed D'oro the reins Bonanza was off at a full gallop the length of the corral. He approached the fence at full speed, and D'oro wondered if he intended to jump it. Instead he whirled around so abruptly, she had to grab the saddle horn to keep from being unseated. Even after Rattlesnake's warning she would not have believed it possible for a horse to turn so fast. They raced back to the front of the barn where Rattlesnake was leaning against the fence with a bootheel hooked over the bottom rail. His hat shoved to the back of his head, he was enjoying watching the girl with her long blond hair streaming behind her, and the horse with his equally blond mane and tail flying in the breeze. One more turn around the corral and D'oro wheeled the horse to a stop in front of the cowboy. Her dancing gray eyes sparkled with excitement as she dismounted and handed the reins back to him.

"I've never ridden a horse like that. Bonanza suits him. He is a golden treasure."

A grin softened Rattlesnake's craggy face as he led the prancing horse back to the stable.

By the time D'oro had showered and changed to a colorful Mexican skirt and a peasant blouse, Annie had returned. D'oro found her on the patio, putting colorful woven placemats on a glass-topped wrought-iron table.

"I thought we'd eat out here. It's such a lovely evening."

"What can I do to help?" D'oro asked as she watched Annie at work. She certainly was striking in crisp dusty-rose-colored linen slacks and a matching print sleeveless open-necked shirt with shades of brown and beige mingling with the same shade of rose. D'oro smiled when the sun caught the small feather of white in Annie's dark hair. She recalled when such markings had been all the rage a few years before and her friends had gone to great lengths with their streaking. None had achieved such dramatic results as that natural color break in Annie's hair. D'oro wondered if it had always been there.

Annie returned D'oro's smile with a warmth that gave animation to her whole classically beautiful face. "Lupe has everything ready. You can help me bring it out."

The previous evening's meal had been planned for a man, but this one was definitely suited to a woman's taste. Halves of ripe avocados were mounded high with chicken salad. They were accompanied by crisp potato chips, which D'oro considered a strictly American treat. For contrast there were juicy tree-ripe pears sprinkled with freshly grated cheese. D'oro could scarcely believe her eyes when Annie removed from the warming oven a plate piled high with plump delicate *sopapillas*, thin squares of deep-fried puffed dough with a hollow center for melted butter and honey. They had been a favorite of D'oro's since she was a small child. Maria always made them on the first night she returned from boarding school. Lime sherbet for dessert and a frosty pitcher of fruity sangría were Lupe's finishing touches of welcome for D'oro. The housekeeper had expressed in her own way her approval of the new-comer from Mexico.

Looking across the table at the beautiful young woman who had so much of her father about her, Annie longed to ask "How is he, how is Jim?" Instead she asked, "Are you familiar with the history of Mariposa?"

"I've read about the explorer John Frémont buying a huge grant from the Mexican government for his Rancho Las Mariposas two years before the discovery of gold in California. Of course I've read about the fantastic fortunes in gold that were taken from the Princeton and the other big mines after the forty-nine Gold Rush. There are some books about it in Dad's library, but I'd love to learn more about it. Did you know my father, Jim Gregg, when he lived here?"

Annie caught her breath sharply. Then she laughed, a bit unsteady at first, but more convincingly as she brought her emotions under control. "In a town the size of Mariposa everyone knows everyone else. Jim was very well liked. What has he told you about living here?"

"Nothing really. He always seemed reluctant to talk about his life before he went to Mexico. Because of my mother, I suppose."

How could Jim have let this girl come back to Mariposa without knowing what she was walking into? Annie thought. Aloud she said, "What did your father think about your coming to Mariposa?"

"He doesn't know I'm here. He's on a mine inspection trip to South America."

"And your mother?" Even after twenty years Annie still found it painful to speak of the woman who was Jim's wife.

"Sally—my mother—only stayed in Mexico about five years, then she left us. My father thought I might visit Sally and her husband in New York while he was gone."

"Your father didn't remarry?" Annie asked in a voice so low, D'oro could barely catch the question.

"No. He has managed to resist the charms of all the senoritas the wives of company officials bring around. When Juan teases him about one who appears particularly interested in him, Dad says, 'A man who can't tell real gold from fool's gold should give up prospecting.'"

There was a long silence while each woman concentrated on her lime sherbet without really tasting it and searched for a way to ask the questions that were uppermost in her mind. Finally it was Annie who asked, "Did your father ever mention me?" Why hadn't he gotten in touch with her?

D'oro searched her memory. "No, I don't think so."

"Why did you come to Mariposa?"

"When I saw Bret's advertisement in the mining journal for someone familiar with the Rodriguez Process, I felt it was somehow meant for me. The return address of Mariposa made it seem like fate."

"How did you know about Mariposa?"

"It was on my birth certificate."

"You weren't named D'oro on your birth certificate, were you?'' Annie asked, making conversation while she tried to find the words for the questions that were uppermost in her mind.

''No. As I said, our housekeeper, Maria, gave me the name when my parents first arrived in Mexico and I was placed in her care. My real name is Sally, but I have never been called anything but D'oro.''

How would she have felt calling this young woman living in her house to whom she had taken such an instant liking by the name Sally? Annie wondered. She was glad she didn't have to find the answer to that question. There were other questions to which she would have to find answers. If D'oro was going to live in Mariposa, Annie felt she should know about the tragedy that had sent Jim into exile in Mexico. Memory of the night when Jim had told her of his decision to go filled her with emptiness and longing that returned after twenty years with a fierceness that mocked all of her attempts to block them out. She busied herself gathering up the dishes, an activity that enabled her to avoid meeting the younger woman's probing eyes.

If Jim hadn't told his daughter about the accident, how could she do so without raising more questions than she had answers for? If Annie didn't tell her, she wondered what the possibilities were of someone else telling her. After so long, only old-timers who were Jim's friends, or his enemies, would know the story. Who of them would draw the connection between him and this pretty young scientist with the same last name? Mariposa was a town that might snicker over the latest gossip, but it still held to the old mining town traditions. A man started fresh with his arrival in town and earned esteem or contempt by his actions there without questions about who he had been or what he had done before he arrived. Did she dare take a chance on that holding true in Jim's case and D'oro's?

Carrying the dishes to the kitchen gave Annie the break in the conversation she needed to try to gather her thoughts. D'oro followed with the rest of the setting. When Annie finished loading the dishwasher, she still had not reached a decision. She stalled for time by asking D'oro about her ride on Bonanza, which Annie had observed as she drove up to the house.

"He's simply marvelous. I never rode a horse who could turn so fast or stop so fast," said D'oro with the enthusiasm of a child.

"That's the hardest part of their training, but those are the skills that make a quarter horse essential for roping either on the range or in a rodeo. I do that part of the training myself," Annie said with pride.

For the rest of the evening they talked about Annie's horses and their training without returning to the unanswered questions revolving in Annie's mind. D'oro went to bed early, and Annie spent a long restless night worrying over the harm that might come to Jim's daughter, who had innocently blundered into the scene of the tragedy Annie's own innocence had set in motion so long ago.

Chapter Three

D'oro's second day at the laboratory was a repetition of the first. Bret's noontime visit was a brief businesslike inquiry as to the progress of her work before he went on to his trailer for lunch. He was still working when she left in the evening. That night D'oro went food shopping.

When Annie went down to the corral after dinner to check on the progress of her injured horse, D'oro returned to the kitchen to prepare her lunch for the next day.

"You don't need to bother with that," Annie protested when she returned. "There isn't that much for Lupe to do and she enjoys cooking."

"So do I," D'oro replied.

"Tired of sandwiches already?"

"I thought something hot might be good. I understand that Thor likes Mexican food." D'oro gave Annie a mischievous smile.

"He sure does. He's a very smart dog." Annie sniffed appreciatively at the inviting smell of chili and grinned her approval.

In the short time she had known her, D'oro

liked Annie better than any woman she had known before. Annie was witty and vivacious with a sophistication and worldly wisdom that D'oro found intriguing.

"I never interrupt a cook when she's being creative. That smell alone could start a stampede." Annie inhaled the fragrance of the simmering meat, chilies, and spices and winked broadly.

The following day when D'oro's watch and the action of the bandanna tied to the cable told her Bret was starting his last load before lunch, she put the pot of chili on the big Bunsen burner. When the pot began to simmer and spicy odor filled the lab, D'oro went to the window. She saw Thor lift his nose and sniff the air appreciatively, then trot over to the laboratory to investigate. By the time Bret's broad shoulders emerged from the shaft, Thor had beat a path between the lab and his usual waiting place.

D'oro saw Bret's head jerk up when the smell reached him, and a puzzled scowl darkened his face as he strode toward the laboratory. After slipping out the door, D'oro waited in the shadow of the building so that she might have the first word.

"Thor and I are having chili for lunch. Would you care to join us?"

Bret looked surprised, then that devastating smile spread across his face slowly. "Give me a few minutes to clean up."

He was back in less time than she expected, looking like a professional man who had just completed a round of golf, rather than a working miner. His thick dark hair gleamed with dampness from the shower. His after-shave lotion seemed to concentrate the fragrance of the pines that surrounded the mine clearing. A blue knit sport shirt hugged his broad shoulders and emphasized the blue of his eyes and the deep bronze of his skin.

D'oro ladled the chili into three bowls when she saw him start toward the lab from his trailer. Bret pulled out one of the two laboratory chairs for her as formally as if they were dining out, rather than eating on her hastily cleared desk.

"When I was at Mines we used to make coffee in a flask over a Bunsen burner when the professor wasn't around, but we never tried to get away with putting one to such full use as this," Bret told her, obviously enjoying the chili as much as Thor, even though he didn't finish his as quickly.

"We eventually had to settle for tea or hot chocolate. *El Profesor* could detect the lingering odor of coffee and would really raise a ruckus." They laughed together, and D'oro found pleasure in their common past experience. For a moment she thought he regarded her more hopefully.

"So your skill at Bunsen burner cookery was acquired later?"

"Yes. Whenever one of *Tia* Maria's kids was sick or she was off helping a neighbor with a new baby, I fixed lunch for *Tio* Juan at the lab. He was very fond of chili."

"All mining men appreciate good food." Bret's manner toward her held the same easy charm he had displayed the first night at Annie's dinner. He flattered her with his eyes and entertained her with amusing anecdotes. He acted as if eating with her in the laboratory were a social event, not a business lunch, putting her in the position of appearing to have had ulterior motives in her invitation if she attempted to turn the conversation toward her work.

When lunch was finished, Bret piled the dishes into the picnic basket in which D'oro had brought them. "Thor and I will do the dishes. We wouldn't want you to think we're male chauvinists."

D'oro started to protest, but she thought of those large competent hands in a pan of soapsuds and smiled. "Does Thor wash or dry?"

"You wouldn't want to know." He gave her a devilish grin as he picked up the basket. He paused at the door long enough to add, "I plan to ride in the morning at eight. Why don't you join me?"

Although D'oro was early, Bret was already waiting in the corral the following morning. Standing beside his big silver-white horse, he smiled his approval when he saw her. A thin cotton shirt molded itself to the contour of her full round breasts, and her well-tailored chino riding pants emphasized her slender hips. She wore a flat black Mexican sombrero with her long blond hair streaming out behind, making her look very young and vulnerable. When Bret's eyes reached her new hand-tooled Mexican boots, his smile disappeared. The boots had been Juan's parting gift to replace her well-worn old ones.

Rattlesnake led Bonanza out of the barn and handed D'oro the reins. As soon as her foot was in the stirrup and her hand on the pommel of the saddle, the horse was off. Anticipating his movement, D'oro was prepared to use the momentum to swing herself into the saddle. At the last minute the slick sole of her new boot slipped. Instead of mounting the horse with a flourish she was left dangling in midair. Bret quickly turned his horse to head off the palomino, as Rattlesnake simply stood and watched. Bonanza stopped as quickly as he had started, dumping D'oro on the ground. It was an indignity that had not happened to her since the day she had tried an eastern saddle at boarding school. She landed beside Bret's horse. Looking up, she could see his look of concern change to a smirk. It took all her control to keep from grabbing some dirt and throwing it in his face.

Bonanza walked over to nuzzle her shoulder. D'oro brushed off the mud and mounted as he stood contrite and docile as a plow horse until she was fully settled in the saddle. What a start for the ride she had been looking forward to all week, she thought ruefully. Rattlesnake opened the corral gate, and the tall man on the big silver horse and the blond girl on the smaller palomino rode out.

The fresh morning air pungent with the scent of pine quickly revived D'oro's good spirits. As they rode through the trees she noticed that Bret was constantly holding back on his larger horse to match his gait to Bonanza's. When D'oro reached an open meadow, she lightly dropped her rein hand on the side of Bonanza's neck, and he immediately demonstrated the qualities for which he had been bred—a burst of speed over a short distance. D'oro leaned forward over the horse's neck, and the wind caught her hair, fluttering it out behind her. With his nose stretched forward and his tail flying in the breeze, the horse was a study in streamlining as he enjoyed the game as much as his rider. Taken by surprise and with his rider's attention focused on something other than a race, the slower-starting big horse was unable to overtake the challenger within the confines of the meadow.

"Never judge a rider by new boots." Bret laughed appreciatively.

Bret's rich natural laugh stirred an answering sensation of pleasure in D'oro. Apparently his chauvinist attitude was limited to their work. He did not show the resentment a Mexican man would at having been beaten by a woman in a race. She liked his sense of humor, the way he could laugh at himself. When she thought about it, she didn't even mind the way he laughed at her. She must have looked comical sitting there in the dirt with the horse nudging her to get up and climb on. That was a different man than she had seen in the laboratory or at dinner. He even looked different, like a wealthy rancher. The new perspective of her employer would definitely be worth getting to know better.

Bret's large horse, Silver, seemed to show a new respect for the palomino and willingly adjusted to his gait as they began to climb the long pine-covered ridge. Beyond a clearing covered with knee-high nut-brown grass Bret reined his horse beside a tortuously shaped manzanita. They looked back into valleys that were mosaics of bronze and yellow fall foliage mingled with the evergreen. It seemed so fresh and unspoiled, D'oro felt as if they were its first discoverers.

"I don't suppose you've ever read any westerns?" Bret asked, almost echoing her thoughts.

"Everything from Zane Grey to Louis L'Amour. My father's library was almost Zacatecas's sole source of books in English. He liked to relax with a western. I didn't realize that some of this land that they described so colorfully a hundred years ago was still so unchanged." She thought how much Bret was like those western heroes— rugged, independent, self-sufficient. He would have been one of the first to explore and, liking what he saw, would have made the land his own. "You're fond of westerns?"

"If you'd care to reread any of the books you mentioned, I'm sure I'd have a copy." He turned Silver toward the crest of the ridge where an even more spectacular panorama spread before them.

A small secluded valley nestled between the ridge they had climbed and the one behind it. They had reached a height overlooking ranks of jagged peaks one behind the other, like ocean waves that finally merged into incredibly blue sky. Bret led the way through the thick pines to the floor of the valley with a familiarity that suggested he went there often. They dismounted and sipped clear spring water from cupped hands, then led their horses down the grassy bank to drink.

"What a beautiful spot! Does it have a name?"

He smiled at her enthusiasm. "It's called Hidden Valley. Would you like to explore it?" He looped the horses' reins so they wouldn't drag while the horses munched the tall grass.

"Shouldn't we tie the horses? It would be a long walk back," she said as he started to walk away and leave them.

"Silver is trained to come when I call him. I don't think Bonanza will wander off, but Silver and I can round him up if he does."

It figured, she thought, that his horse would be trained to come when he called. Voicing her speculation, she asked, "And your women, are they trained to come when you call them?"

"I'm working on it," he said, giving her a crooked mischievous grin.

Taking her hand, he led her along the bank of the swiftly rushing stream through a grove of cottonwood and willow. The shade felt cool and inviting after their long ride, but the sensation that started in the hand Bret was holding was warm and tingling, as though it were a warning.

From the shade of the grove they emerged suddenly into bright sunlight in a natural amphitheater surrounded by rugged pine-clad mountains. D'oro breathed deeply, inhaling the thin, pure pine-scented mountain air.

"It's perfect. I never dreamed there was still such unspoiled beauty here. I could stay in such a spot forever."

"But then, like a woman, you'd want to build a house, and what would happen to your unspoiled beauty?'' he teased. His voice showed no trace of the antagonism his words suggested.

"It wouldn't need to spoil it if it was a rambling ranch-style house built of these big logs we see all around us. It should have a huge fireplace built of this native stone, and a hand-hewed beam ceiling.''

"Not a white adobe with a red tile roof? I thought you admired Annie's house so much.''

"Not here. Houses, like people, should be at home with their surroundings.'' Though she sensed he was teasing her, she felt too strongly about the matter to take it lightly.

"Where would you put this dream house, in the middle of the clearing?''

Then she definitely felt she was being either tested or baited. D'oro looked carefully at the valley in all directions as if she were actually selecting the site for her imagined home.

"I think I'd build on top of that little rise by the big boulder at the edge of the trees.'' She indicated a spot at the back of the clearing. As they walked toward the place she had suggested she felt as if they were pioneers exploring land to be homesteaded. He was no longer holding her hand, but as they walked his fingers brushed hers, sending sparks like static electricity through her. There was a magnetism about Bret that seemed to trigger a response in D'oro whenever he was near her.

They climbed a grassy knoll at the base of the boulder. Her judgment had been correct. The entire valley spread before them like a three-dimensional painting. In the lower corner their two horses grazed by the stream.

"I approve of your selection. You have a good feel for the nature of the land. Would you care to sit a spell on your front stoop?" he asked with a good imitation of a western drawl.

D'oro laughed and sat down beside Bret on an outcropping of rock at the edge of the rise. His arm went around her, but it was more of a companionable gesture than romantic. Still, it made her wonder what it would be like to be kissed by Bret, who was so different from any man she had known before. They sat and silently enjoyed the rare peace of their beautiful isolated retreat.

A small animal startled the horses down by the stream. "Does your plan include corrals for horses?"

"Not if you train all the horses to come when you call them," she teased.

With that crooked grin that wrought such a change in his rugged features, he put two fingers in his mouth and emitted a long piercing whistle. Silver's head jerked up and he galloped toward them in long easy strides, his mane and tail flying in the breeze like Pegasus loping across the heavens. Reacting as if it were a race, Bonanza charged hard in pursuit of the stallion. The action of the horses made the whole panorama look like a carefully composed motion picture scene.

When the cottonwood grove through which they had walked hid the horses from view, Bret got to his feet and helped D'oro up. He hesitated a moment, as if thinking about something, then turned and walked down the grassy knoll with ease. As D'oro followed behind him the slick soles of her new boots again betrayed her, sending her sliding down the slope to crash into Bret's outstretched arms. Although she threw up her hands to cushion the impact, her body met his hard muscular chest with bruising force.

"You come without being called. I like that," he said, laughing with a deep earthy sound that made his chest vibrate beneath her flushed cheek. Her heart was pounding as wildly as if she had fallen from a great height. His arms closed around her, holding her feet above the ground as if she had deliberately thrown herself at him and he had caught her. She felt weightless and giddy with a sensation of still falling through empty space. He slowly let her down until her toes touched the ground while his powerful arms held her slender form pressed tight against his lean hard body. His lips descended, touching hers lightly, teasingly. Then his mouth became masterful, exploring, questioning. Her pulse pounded at her temples and echoed in the hollow of her throat. Desire such as she had never known in her well-monitored life flamed through her. The slow caressing motion of his hands cupping her breasts brought a feeling of exquisite pleasure.

That was not the way a caballero would have kissed her after such brief acquaintance. In the old-world class-conscious society in which she had been raised, men flattered women prodigiously and engaged in outrageous flirtation. However, they approached the daughter of a powerful man like Senor Griegos with cautious restraint. Bret had paid her no compliments, had not indicated that he liked or admired her in any way. There had been no words of endearment or signs of affection before he kissed her in such an intimate way. What did he really feel? Was he merely amusing himself with her? His mouth continued to explore the softness of hers. Her instincts directed her to respond to him with the fervor she felt, but her confused mind dictated restraint. She hesitated, and the moment was lost.

Bret raised his head and searched her face with hooded eyes. Then he picked her up as if she were a child and set her on her waiting horse. He mounted his horse in a single fluid motion and started up the trail. Watching the easy set of his broad shoulders, D'oro knew she would never understand Bret—the chameleon who changed his mood according to his background. He didn't even like having her around the mine or the laboratory, yet there in the secluded valley his actions spoke of wanting to make love to her. Was he again testing the talents of the newcomer? If so, it was a test she knew she had failed quite miserably.

D'oro felt lost and alone in a strange new world, playing a game the rules of which she didn't understand. Trying to sort out her tangled emotions, D'oro allowed her horse to lag behind as she followed Bret back to the ranch in stony silence.

Chapter Four

Bret's Monday noon check-in at the laboratory emphasized how completely he separated his work and his personal life. It was as if the Saturday ride had never happened.

"How's it going?" he asked, a question so routine, D'oro almost winced each day when he asked it.

"So far just the way it should. The gold and silver dissolved in solution. The quartz, lead, and other base metals remained firm. Of course, I don't have zinc pellets to cause the gold and silver to drop out again." She smiled as she remembered what Juan called his magic. With the flourishes of a magician he would drop the zinc into the solution in which the precious metals had been suspended and watch her delighted young face as the silver began to take form again on the bottom of the container.

"I'm running short of dynamite. Why don't we go to Dry Gulch today and get the things we need?"

The suggestion delighted D'oro. She was anxious to have the materials to complete her work, and a small ray of optimism within her suggested it might be an opportunity to recapture some of the moments of their shared companionship before the concluding disaster on Saturday.

"I'm afraid the lady has priority. You'll have to stay home today," Bret told Thor as he pranced impatiently beside the pickup when preparations for the trip had been completed.

"I could lose a good friend that way," D'oro said as the dog eyed her apprehensively. "Bring him along if he won't crowd you."

Bret opened the passenger door for her and then allowed Thor to bound in through the driver's door as was his custom. D'oro had assumed the dog would sit between them, but he stepped majestically across her lap and pressed his nose possessively against the side window. D'oro wasn't about to acknowledge her error, so she slid obligingly to the center of the seat. When Bret started the pickup and turned to back out of the parking place, his lean hard thigh pressed against her, igniting an awareness of him throughout her whole being. It could be a very difficult day, D'oro mused. Bret showed no awareness of the contact between them, but he must have noticed her sharp intake of breath, her tense reaction to his touch.

"We'll take Highway Forty-nine today. It follows the route of the gold seekers through the Mother Lode country," he said when they reached the main road and turned to circle the base of pine-covered Mt. Bullion. At the weathered sign for Mt.

Ophir he turned onto a dirt road and parked beside a crumbling structure of stone and weathered wood. They walked together toward the historic site.

"This was the old Mount Ophir mint, which made fifty dollar hexagonal gold pieces in 1850 under a government agreement for private minting."

"You don't suppose there is still a sample that might have slipped through the cracks of this floor?" she asked, looking down at the heavy ship's planking she was standing on.

"No chance. Those old miners were a lot more efficient than we give them credit for. Such a piece would be worth a fortune today, but when they were minted, fifty dollars was a lot of money even in a gold camp. You can be sure they were carefully accounted for. I enjoy imagining myself part of the gold rush days."

D'oro wasn't sure she would have liked a woman's part of a gold rush camp, but she was delighted that the day was to be an adventure, not merely a business trip.

When they returned to the car, Thor was satisfied that his claim had been established and curled up at D'oro's feet and went to sleep. With mingled relief and regret she moved away from Bret to watch the passing countryside out the passenger window, making it easier to maintain her composure.

Highway '49 climbed through rugged mountains marked by quartz outcroppings and tailings from abandoned mines.

"Apparently, that mine isn't abandoned," said D'oro, pointing to a crude sign recently painted in red atop a barbed-wire fence: TRESPASSERS WILL BE SHOT ON SIGHT—THE NALTONS.

"Just like the old days of claim jumpers and vigilantes," Bret agreed with a rich chuckle that reverberated deep inside D'oro.

The next sharp bend in the road brought them into the small mining town of Coulterville. Unlike the ghost mining towns they had passed, the relic of a bygone day was in active use. A spreading live oak tree stood in the center of Coulterville's main street.

"The town's Hangman's Tree. Every mining camp had one," he said as he parked beside Whistling Billy, a small locomotive that had once hauled ore from the Mary Harrison Mine to the stamp mill over the "crookedest railroad in the world."

The three-story pioneer Jeffrey Hotel dominated the cluster of ancient frame structures. On the wooden veranda that extended out over the plank sidewalk sat two white-bearded men wearing flannel shirts and high laced boots.

As they crossed the street Bret waved a greeting to the two old miners. "This time of year the country store has fresh apple cider. Shall we try a jug, or would you like something stronger?" He nodded toward the gaudy entrance of the old saloon.

"Cider sounds great. We don't often find it in Mexico."

The country store was an incredible jumble of

merchandise, from gold pans and mining picks to space-age plastic gadgets. Bret told the bald rotund owner what they wanted, and from the back room he produced a frosty jug of cider and a package of plastic cups.

Bret led the way to a bench on the hotel veranda facing the two ancient miners. He filled his cup and D'oro's, then holding up the jug asked, "Care to join us?"

The closer of the miners hesitated as if such a drink might damage his standing, then yielded to the lure of the frosty amber liquid.

"Thanks, son. It is getting a mite hot. I'm Hawkeye Walker, and this here is Joshua Brown."

"Bret Johnson and D'oro Gregg," Bret acknowledged, filling cups for the two old men.

"Bet your pa was one of them eastern dudes read Bret Harte's stories about the minin' camp 'n' named his son for the dream he never got around to."

Bret laughed and nodded, although the miner's time frame was warped and it had been his grandfather who had first selected the name.

"D'oro, that's Spanish for made out of gold. You come from Mexico?"

"Yes. Zacatecas."

"That's silver country. Lot of the early miners around here were Mexicans, named places like Sonora and Hornitos. Hear that's mighty rough country down there."

"Not as rough as Coulterville, I guess. They don't shoot trespassers on sight—always talk to them real polite first," prodded D'oro.

The old miner's laugh was almost a cackle. "Reckon you mean the Nalton boys' sign. Mean enough to tell the Devil how to run hell, that bunch. Ugly as sin, too, all except the youngest one, Clay, and he went off down to Mariposa, courtin' the Baxter girl after her pa found the big silver strike and Baxter got himself killed in an automobile."

"Never thought there was silver in this gold country until Baxter started pullin' it out clear down there at the end of the Mother Lode," added his friend Joshua.

"Didn't do Clay Nalton much good," continued Hawkeye, ignoring the interruption. "The gal only got half the mine from her pa, and Clay got himself killed for that. Can't say it was much of a loss. Folks thought the rest of the Nalton boys would raise real, hell down in Mariposa 'bout Clay's death. There was some talk, then the whole thing just sort'a died away. You two from around Mariposa?" Hawkeye nodded in the direction from which they had come.

"We're just tenderfeet from down near Mariposa," Bret answered evasively. "Looks like there's quite a bit of action around Coulterville," he continued, turning the conversation back to the old-timers.

"A little mining, but mostly fishermen from over Lake McClure, since they put in the new dam and flooded over the old mill site. 'Course we get a lot of amateur prospectors in the summer with the price of gold the way it is, but it ain't like the old days." Hawkeye paused to gulp his cider.

D'oro could sense the pleasure Bret took in the tales the two miners began to tell as each tried to top the other with reminiscences enriched by faulty memory. Though the stories of the old miners might be only gossip turned into legend, those about the fantastic quantities of gold taken from some of the surrounding mines a hundred years before were quite real, documented in the records of Wells Fargo and the old courthouses.

"We're going up to Dry Gulch, so I guess we better get started," Bret finally said.

"Good to meet you, young fellow. Thanks for the cider. Nice name, D'oro, fits you, too," and the old miner laughed with his odd cackling sound.

When they were back in the pickup and had given Thor his share of the cider, D'oro voiced the question that had been troubling her. "I wonder why Annie married a man like Clay Nalton if he was as bad as they say he was?"

"I don't know. She never mentions him. Hawkeye was probably exaggerating. These old miners tell everything bigger than life."

"I suppose you're right," she agreed, still disturbed by the information and its suggestion of past sorrow for Annie. D'oro pushed the thought to the back of her mind, determined that nothing should interfere with the day of rare companionship with Bret.

The road beyond Coulterville was as steep and tortuous as the one approaching it, with more quartz outcroppings and old mine tailings.

"Were you really named for Bret Harte?" she asked him, smiling.

"Those old miners have lost track of the passage of time. My father was named for Bret Harte, and the name was passed on to me. Are you familiar with his stories?"

"There were some of Bret Harte's books in Dad's library. They were well read. He seemed to be fond of them. I particularly liked his 'The Luck of Roaring Camp.' This is the country he wrote about, isn't it?"

"Yes. Both Bret Harte and Mark Twain wrote about this great rugged land and the men who answered its challenge." His hand swept toward jagged forested peaks that stretched to the horizon on D'oro's side of the road.

Thor climbed up on the seat in front of the window to see what had attracted their interest. Bret turned to speak to Thor as D'oro moved over until her rounded hips pressed against his lean hard thigh. A flicker of amusement danced in his eyes. He stretched his arm along the back of the seat, the shift of his broad shoulders making ample room on the seat for the three of them. He smiled at her tense reaction to the physical contact between them.

"Relax. I won't bite."

"I thought Thor might if I infringed on his claim." D'oro managed to keep her voice light, although she was acutely aware of the power and magnetism emanating from Bret through all the places where their bodies touched. Like the old miners, here was a man who would meet any challenge eagerly.

"Thor is a perfect gentleman. He never bites a lady who doesn't bite first."

The way he was looking at her, she wasn't sure Bret had any such scruples. D'oro leaned back, allowing her head to roll into the hollow of his shoulder. She could feel the warm smooth skin beneath his thin cotton shirt, and inviting curls of dark hair peeked into its open V. Bret's hand slid down her arm and his eyes were focused on her lips. She could almost feel the warm pressure of his mouth on hers.

After he bent down and brushed her lips lightly with his, Bret returned his hand to the steering wheel and braked to a near stop. D'oro could feel her heart pound in anticipation that he intended to stop and do a more thorough job of kissing her.

He turned the pickup sharply to the right onto a graveled road she hadn't noticed. "Here we are," he said as they bumped along the unpaved road, raising a cloud of dust behind them.

D'oro didn't know where they were, but it certainly wasn't a lovers' lane. She felt like they were actors in a play on which the curtain had fallen and that they were back in their workday world. She also had an uneasy feeling that she didn't really understand the role she was supposed to play, and even less the one Bret was playing.

The weatherbeaten sign DRY GULCH seemed to be part of a western stage set until she remembered it was the location of the mining outfitter. "Is this where you get your supplies?" D'oro asked in amazement.

"Only mining outfitter still operating in this part of California. Been in business here almost a hundred years."

The stock inside the old stone warehouse was modern and varied. Bret ordered three cases of dynamite, and D'oro added zinc pellets and nitric and hydrochloric acids.

"Having any success with aqua regia?" the man who was waiting on them asked, looking up from the order form.

"I won't know for sure until I have the zinc pellets to complete the process," D'oro answered.

The man looked surprised that it was the pretty blond woman and not Bret who answered his question. "I'll have to see your blasting permit again," he told Bret. He totaled up the order and noted the number of the permit Bret handed him on the inventory opposite the order for dynamite.

"Hope you don't mind riding in a truck carrying dynamite," Bret prodded when the man left them to fill the order.

"Not if you don't mind driving one hauling acid," she countered.

"Should be no trouble as long as we don't let them work together," he answered with a tone that suggested he was talking about more than acid and dynamite.

The message was quite clear: They would keep their personal lives separate from their business relationship. The charm that seemed so much a part of Bret in other situations did not affect his doubts about D'oro's professional competence.

When they returned to the pickup, the air of a shared holiday had completely disappeared. It was a long subdued drive back along the route that had been so fascinating that morning.

The sun was disappearing behind the backdrop of the mountains when they reached the ranch.

"Thank you for a lovely day. This is enchanting country," she told him when he helped her out of the pickup and walked with her to the door. It was the first time D'oro had found the front door locked, but it was after Lupe's regular quitting time. She dug in her purse for the key Annie had given her. Bret took it from her fingers and unlocked the heavy oak door. She smiled up at him and she thought he was going to kiss her. This time she would not be caught by surprise. He hesitated a moment, then reached out and opened the door.

"Won't you come in?" she invited. "I'm sure Lupe has left the fixings for a Mexican dinner that would please Thor, and there's always enough to feed a family."

Again he hesitated. For a man who usually made rapid-fire decisions, he seemed to be having uncharacteristic difficulty making up his mind. "Guess I'd better not, but I'll take a rain check on it. I—I should unload that stuff before dark."

It was clearly an excuse, and not a very convincing one. D'oro knew that there were plenty of outdoor spotlights so that unloading in the dark would be no problem. If he didn't want to have

dinner with her, why didn't he just say so? She
would simply never understand him.

"I won't be working in the morning. I have—
uh—a business appointment," Bret mumbled.
"Why don't you take the morning off? It's been a
long day."

"I've enjoyed every minute of it," she assured
him. When he did not respond, she added, "It
would be good to sleep in, thanks." Quietly she
entered the house and closed the door behind
her, venting her frustration by the vicious way she
kicked off her shoes before going to the kitchen
for a lonely snack.

D'oro did not sleep late. She had experienced a
night of panoramic dreams about the gold rush
days. Somehow the miner in each scene had a
startling resemblance to Bret. She awakened at the
usual time with the feeling that she had something important to do that day, then she remembered that she had the chemicals to complete her
experiment. The thought of finishing her work
and leaving Mariposa made her feel empty.

The morning matched D'oro's lonely mood.
Gray clouds scudded across the blue sky when she
walked to the corral for an early morning ride. Annie was still in town at a meeting, but at least
Bonanza greeted her eagerly. That morning the
fast start and flying mount worked perfectly. The
brisk wind sweeping the hair back from her face
and the smooth rhythmic gait of the horse re-
stored D'oro's good spirits. She turned toward the
lower pasture where hints of fall color were beginning to brighten the stream bank. When she

reached the boundary of the S/S, the wind had risen to a gale. Dust devils sprang up and twisted across the brown pasture. The wind whipped her long hair across her face and stung her eyes.

"Guess it just isn't my day for a ride," she said aloud to the horse as if her words, not the gentle touch of the rein hand on his neck, caused him to turn back to the ranch.

From her father, D'oro had learned the calming, healing power of work. The sight of silver dropping into the bottom of the flask from Juan's magic combination would bring pleasure. It was late enough that Bret would have left for his appointment, and that was just as well. She shrugged in a manner she had copied as a child from Maria.

The wind was still gusting when D'oro parked her Volkswagen in its accustomed place among the trees at what Bret jokingly called the mine's front door. She paused a moment to watch the bright flashes of color of a swarm of golden monarch butterflies clinging to one of the pines. They fluttered there as if giving grace and beauty were enough to expect of life.

As she emerged from the trees D'oro ducked her head to protect her eyes from the stinging bite of wind and dust. She was well into the clearing before she saw the small bright red sports car with a Nevada license plate parked beside Bret's pickup. She had not expected his appointment to be at the mine or she would not have gone there until afternoon as he suggested, but it was too late then. Anyone watching from the trailer would already have seen her. There really was no reason why her work in the lab should interfere with Bret's business at the trailer, anyhow. She would enjoy presenting him with the completed work earlier than he anticipated.

As D'oro expected, he had put the chemicals in their proper place the previous evening when he unloaded them. She was so busy assembling the equipment for her work, she did not notice Bret's approach until he spoke.

"D'oro, is everything all right?"

"Yes. I just got impatient to be sure the zinc would work, and it was too windy to ride," she said defensively.

"Bret, we'll be late," called a petulant feminine voice.

Bret turned, and D'oro found herself being measured by the hostile violet eyes of a stylishly dressed platinum blonde a few years older than herself.

"D'oro Gregg, this is Candy Stevens." Bret introduced them without enthusiasm.

"I'm pleased to meet you," D'oro responded, watching to see if the other girl offered her hand. She did not.

"It's a real pleasure," answered Candy with a stilted accent strange to D'oro's ears. To Bret, she added with a flutter of long eyelashes, "We could postpone our plans if something important has come up."

"No," he answered hesitantly, "I can see the results tomorrow," and he followed Candy's calculatedly enticing walk back to her car, which he drove.

D'oro plumped down in the chair at her work-bench, her enthusiasm for the project having vanished like dew on a summer morning. So that was his business appointment, she thought, tears stinging her eyelids. She had been naive as a schoolgirl to think their mutual love of horses and the shared pleasure of rambling through the historic gold country had any special significance for him. Again Maria's words came back to haunt her: "A man can't think of you as *bella señorita* and a lady metallurgist at the same time." Not that Maria would approve of Candy. In the colonial Mexican society in which Maria still believed, there were only good women and bad women. But D'oro had long ago realized that good or bad simply did not apply to beautiful women like Candy or her own mother, any more than they did to the butterflies, *las mariposas,* for which the area was named. When Sally left them, D'oro recalled, it had been better for both the little girl and her father. It was as if he had let a beautiful butterfly out of its cage so they would no longer have to watch it beat its wings against the bars.

D'oro understood why Bret made lame excuses about not staying for dinner and went racing back to the mine. Candy was waiting. Bret had his pretty butterfly, too, and he could keep her for all D'oro cared. She would just complete her work, give him his precious formula, and go—she wasn't sure where, but go. She didn't want to go back to Zacatecas without finding that indefinable part of herself for which she was searching, yet she certainly hadn't found it in Mariposa. "You might visit your mother in New York while I'm gone," her father had suggested when he left for the mine inspection trip to South America.

Instinctively D'oro knew that whatever she was seeking was not in New York with Sally and her new husband. It was odd she still thought of her unknown stepfather that way, although he and Sally had been married for twelve years.

When she had taken the job, D'oro had hoped she might feel complete in her work, but she had reckoned without Bret's rejection of her in her job and then as a woman. At least she should be able to put that behind her soon enough. She went to her workbench and carefully weighed zinc pellets and poured them into the flask of murky liquid in which silver particles were suspended in their acid extractor. She watched as the zinc drifted down through the liquid and settled on the bottom of the flask, but Juan's miracle did not occur. There were no shiny particles of silver following the zinc. She tried again. Agitating the flask gently, she watched and waited, but nothing happened. She picked up a glass rod and stirred the mixture vigorously and watched the settling intently—nothing!

D'oro slumped back in her chair, lowered her head on her workbench, and dissolved in the tears that had been threatening since Bret followed Candy out of the laboratory. When the emotional storm subsided, she focused her attention on the unresponsive flask. She had been so sure it would work. She had proceeded so carefully. Where had she gone wrong? She was glad she was alone when the failure came, but the next day she would have to tell Bret. How could she face him?

She sat listlessly for several minutes, then began to clear up the laboratory. Unless she could find some error she would simply have to start over, but this was not the day for it. When everything was back in its place, she walked disconsolately to her car. As she opened the car door she noted that in spite of the clouds overhead she had neglected to roll up the window. *It's a wonder it didn't rain. That would have been all I needed,* she thought bitterly.

The wind was still gusting so strong, it took all of D'oro's concentration to keep the light car on the road as she drove back to the ranch. As she braked to a stop in the driveway there was a thump on the floor behind her seat, and a large black head appeared over her shoulder, lapping lovingly at her earlobe.

"Thor!" She hugged the beautiful dog, knowing she really should scold him. His happy bark as he followed her out of the car brought Annie from the corral.

"Where's Bret?" she asked, a note of alarm in her voice.

"He has an appointment," D'oro answered with sarcasm as she used Bret's description of the day. "A blonde in a red sports car with a Nevada license plate. Thor must have climbed in my open window after they left. I didn't know he was there until we got to the ranch."

"I always did think animals have more sense than people. He doesn't like Candy. She's too fanatical about her clothes to let Thor near her. Besides, she can't ride a horse," Annie added as if that were the ultimate condemnation. "And what are you going to do about him?" Annie asked.

"I think they will be gone awhile, but I just can't take my friend here back and risk running into them again." D'oro covered her mouth with her hand, aware of how completely she had revealed her feelings about Bret.

"Thor wasn't the him I was talking about, either," said Annie pointedly. "I thought you were the kind of woman who would fight for what she wants."

Annie's words conjured up in D'oro's mind the street fights she had seen between Mexican peasant women over the attentions of a man. She slowly shook her head.

"You're going to be a lady if it kills you, or breaks your heart.... I made that mistake once. He was a lot like Bret," she added so low that D'oro could barely catch her words. "Things might have been so different," murmured Annie as she turned abruptly and walked away.

D'oro stared after the older woman in surprise. She remembered what the miner in Coulterville had said about her husband and wondered if there was any connection between his gossip and Annie's advice.

Chapter Five

D'oro was playing catch with Thor when Annie walked out of the house, her manner once more calm and self-assured. She had changed into an expensively tailored sage-green pantsuit. The effect was softened by a silk print blouse in a coordinating color.

"I have to go into Mariposa. How about going with me? You might enjoy looking around the museum."

D'oro hesitated and glanced at the frolicking dog.

"Rattlesnake is going up to check the north pasture fence to see that the wind didn't blow that old cottonwood down on it. He can drop your friend off at the mine. Thor stays there without any problem if someone takes the time to tell him to guard the shaft. Bret must have been in a rush when he left. I suppose Candy was in a hurry to get back to the city."

D'oro wondered if Rattlesnake's errand had been contrived to relieve her of the problem of Thor. She was sure the remark about Candy was meant to assure her that there was no danger of running into Bret and Candy in Mariposa.

"I'd love to go if you can wait a minute while I change."

"No hurry, but you're fine in your slacks and blouse. Mariposa is a blue jeans and boots town." Glancing down at her own expensive outfit, Annie added with amusement, "I let my lawyer intimidate me into getting all spruced up. He's the only man in town who wears a business suit."

"I'd feel better if I changed," D'oro answered, and Annie smiled her understanding.

Rattlesnake pulled his battered pickup to a stop beside them and opened the door. Thor accepted the invitation with a bound and settled beside the small man as if they were old friends.

After catching sight of her lusterless eyes and tense face in the mirror, D'oro selected a bright cherry-red sweater in the hopes of at least having some reflected color. With it she wore tailored navy-blue slacks that fit her trim figure perfectly. She ran a brush through her long blond hair and applied a dash of her brightest lipstick.

Annie's silver-gray Porsche was so right for her, D'oro thought, sleek, sophisticated, yet young in spirit. As she drove the familiar road with ease Annie unobtrusively studied the young woman sitting so tense and miserable beside her. When Candy first appeared on the scene and Bret began flaunting their relationship before the bemused townspeople, Annie had been relieved. It had stilled the gossip that had arisen from her deal with the handsome young miner and the property she had previously refused to sell. Then in the curious re-enactment of her own youth in the person of the young woman sitting silently beside her, Annie knew the pain that Candy's presence caused.

"How are you and Bonanza getting along?" Annie asked, breaking the oppressive silence.

"He's the most beautiful horse I have ever ridden," D'oro answered with enthusiasm.

"You seem to have made quite a conquest. Ride him as if he were your own, whenever you have time. It will be good for him."

And for me, too, she means, D'oro thought, noting the concern in Annie's voice.

"Where did you go on your ride Saturday?"

"Hidden Valley." Annie gave D'oro a quick appraising glance as the younger woman continued, "Do you happen to know who owns it?"

"Hidden Valley was to have been my wedding present from my father, but when my parents were killed, I inherited the entire ranch."

D'oro was sorry to have unknowingly recalled memories that were so painful to Annie.

"I hadn't been up there in years. Bret was so anxious to buy it when he sold his first silver shipment that I agreed."

Bret owned Hidden Valley! He had been baiting her. How it must have amused him to hear her fantasize about her dream house on property he owned. What a naive child she must have seemed to him compared to Candy. After what had happened today, she wished she never had to see him again. If only she didn't have to go back to the laboratory. That was one thing Juan would not tolerate in all the years he had encouraged and trained her—to give up on a piece of research because the first effort was disappointing. She sighed. Then the other part of what Annie had said registered in her mind. "Bret is shipping his ore?"

"Yes. He found a very rich vein of silver that he ships to the smelter in Arizona. It would be more profitable with his own processing mill, but I think he has more than that in mind. A mill would give new life to the whole area just as my father's operations did during the Depression."

So that was Bret's ambition, not only a profitable mine but a mill, a home in Hidden Valley, and a position of leadership in the community. In everything he did Bret was a man who knew what he wanted and went after it. Unfortunately, the same seemed to be true of what he did not want, and he did not want her in his business or in the home she knew he would one day build in Hidden Valley.

D'oro stared rigidly ahead of her as the powerful car purred smoothly down the hill into the bowl where Mariposa sits, surrounded by mountains on all sides. The one-street business section had a pioneer feeling, as newer buildings had been designed to blend with the character of the older ones. Overhanging porches sheltered wooden sidewalks in front of natural cedar and split rock buildings. The white adobe Schlageter Hotel dominated the center of town, where wagon wheels and other western symbols were used for atmosphere. Businesses had such names as Lucky Strike Produce, Gold Coin Bar, and Wagon Wheel and Sugar Pine restaurants.

"I love these old mining towns," D'oro said with an attempt at cheerfulness.

Annie pulled to a stop in front of a low rambling ranch-style building at the head of the main street, which was identified as the museum and library. "I should be back by four," Annie said, checking her watch.

"No hurry. I've been wanting to see the museum," D'oro answered, remembering Bret's enthusiasm. She had hoped he would show it to her, but the show that occupied him that day was the one he had rushed off to with Candy, she thought bitterly. Trying to banish thoughts of Bret from her mind, she walked determinedly through the exhibits. Scale-model shop windows large enough to hold life-size mannequins depicted scenes of Mariposa's early days. Pages from a gold seeker's diary provided the keynote of the exhibits, starting with a chest containing flour, horseshoe nails, and other essentials for the prairie crossing. The miner's cabin had only a crude table and a bunk of log poles laced together with leather thongs in the corner by the fireplace. A wooden Mexican gold pan was displayed between Chinese herbal medicines and Irish whiskey as contributions of waves of miners from around the world.

The window of Trabucco's Emporium was a startling contrast to the austerity of the other displays. It held plumed fans, satin waistcoats, a velvet coat and large velvet hats, and women's high laced shoes. After the lonely drudgery of the mines, the gold seekers seemed to like their women fancy and frivolous—and apparently they still did, D'oro thought miserably. Acutely conscious of how alone she was, D'oro turned back toward the library.

Beside a woodburning Comstock stove she saw the safe that had started Bret on the quest that ended in his buying the Heartbreaker Mine. Protected by heavy plate glass, the ancient safe contained a small gold pan with more than an ounce of gold flakes. Next to it were samples of natural gold leaf of such artistic free-form design that it looked like a goldsmith had designed them. A white quartz rock looked like it was topped with a modernistic gold bird. Other quartz rocks contained gleaming ladybugs of gold. There were solid gold nuggets resembling intricately carved buttons. In the lower corner of the display was a piece of silver-encrusted quartz of the same type but far richer than those D'oro had been working with in the lab. She studied the inscription under the specimen: "Sample of silver ore assaying over 200 ounces per ton, taken from the Silver Queen Mine in 1960 by Franklin Baxter and Jim Gregg—Donated by Annie Baxter."

D'oro stared at the words in disbelief. The mine in which her father had been a partner was the Silver Queen. He had been a partner with Annie's father, Franklin Baxter, and later with Annie and her husband. Why hadn't Annie said so? D'oro had felt a greater affection growing for the older woman than for anyone in her life, except her father. In some ways she felt closer to Annie than to Maria, and Annie seemed to return her feelings. When D'oro had asked Annie about her father, she had said she knew him and spoke favorably about him, but she had not indicated that there had been a close association between them. Perhaps there had been trouble between Annie and her mother. Annie had spoken guardedly of Sally. She also seemed reluctant to talk about the Silver Queen, but her husband, whom she had never mentioned, was killed in the mine cave-in.

D'oro studied the rock intently as if its mirrorlike surface could reveal more about the past. In vain she searched her memory for any additional information, any clues. Though Sally had been restive and unhappy before she left, D'oro couldn't remember any fights between her parents in which there had been hurled accusations. After Sally was gone, her father had never talked about Mariposa. Of course, he hadn't known she was going there, so the names of people and places from his life there would have been meaningless.

D'oro knew she could simply tell Annie what she had found out and ask about her father and their partnership in the Silver Queen. She feared the questions would be awkward and painful in view of the way Annie had avoided the subject. She wondered if there was someone less involved who might tell her about the Silver Queen.

Slowly she approached the desk of the librarian, a studious-looking middle-aged woman with keen dark eyes behind horn-rimmed glasses.

"Can you tell me anything about the gold and silver displays in the old safe?"

The woman shook her head. "No more than what's printed on the display cards. The exhibits were already in place when I came here six years ago. We have several books on the California Gold Rush that include details and descriptions of local mines. Did the exhibit you were interested in come from one of the 1850 discoveries?"

"No. The mine was a later discovery, opened during the Depression, I believe."

"No one has compiled a history of the later discoveries. Owners are sometimes reluctant to give too many details. Significant finds were usually reported at the time in the weekly *Mariposa Gazette*."

"Do you have a file of back copies of the *Gazette*?"

"No, but there's a complete file in the county clerk's office in the courthouse. They're open until five."

Automatically D'oro glanced at her watch. Annie wouldn't be back for an hour, and the courthouse was only a few blocks away. In fact, nothing in Mariposa was more than a few blocks away, she thought absently.

The two-story white frame courthouse proudly displayed the date 1854, when it was built in the style of a New England town hall. It had later been completed with a steeple, a clock, and black shutters. The entry was filled with glass showcases of colorful mineral samples from local mines, but those did not have the value of the ones in the museum safe. D'oro thought it was odd that when Bret told her about the silver sample in the safe that Annie had donated, he had not mentioned that Jim Gregg had been listed as one of the mine owners. D'oro promised herself she would go back another time and examine the lesser mineral samples to see if any of them offered a clue as to why Juan's formula didn't work.

Just beyond a display of the unique cattle brands that had been used in the county since 1853 she found the county clerk's office. A friendly middle-aged woman brought a large green-covered book from the vault and placed it on a table in response to her request.

"Funny, there hasn't been a request for these papers in fifteen years, now all of a sudden you're the second person in a week to ask for them. Bet someone is thinking of opening up one of the old claims." She gave D'oro a knowing wink.

Was Bret the other person who had been interested in the Silver Queen and its tragic history? If so, why at this particular time?

In 1955 the *Mariposa Gazette* had been a six-page weekly that was published on Thursdays and sold for seven cents. The masthead proclaimed that it had been published since 1854 and was "California's Oldest Weekly of Continuous Publication." The paper was devoted completely to local items without blazing headlines or concern with the events of the outside world. The front page contained such items as "Mt. Gaines Mine Is Sold," "Rattlesnake Bites El Portal Youngster," "Cow-Belles Beef Dinner for Valentine Day," and "Benefit for Volunteer Firemen." Advertisements for Kelly's Korner Store offered saltines for twenty-five cents and tomatoes two pounds for twenty-three cents.

Unfamiliar with small-town newspapers, D'oro was fascinated and amused by the type of news the *Gazette* printed. In boldface type the front page of the March 15, 1955 issue carried the information she was looking for: NEW FIND AT THE SILVER QUEEN. She quickly read the short item reporting that Franklin Baxter and his young partner, Jim Gregg, had opened up a rich new vein at the Silver Queen, which had been discovered by Baxter in 1932. The article expressed the hope that the find might be part of a new mining boom for Mariposa County. The story confirmed what D'oro had seen in the museum, but added no new information.

After a little practice, D'oro found she could flip from one issue to the next and quickly scan the front page, but succeeding weeks provided no more information about the Silver Queen. Either the operation was very secretive or the vein had not been as large as originally hoped.

On November 22 of the same year the upper left column, which was reserved for the week's most important news, told of the death of Franklin and Margaret Baxter in an automobile crash. The obituary related that Franklin Baxter had come to Mariposa as a Depression-days gold seeker and found a rich strike at the Silver Queen. It told of his buying the Sterling Silver Ranch and hiring local artisans and craftsmen to build the hacienda. It listed his many civic offices and honors. The term "one of Mariposa's leading citizens" seemed well deserved. His wife, Margaret, had been a leader of social and charity groups. Their only survivor was their daughter, Ann.

At that time Annie would have been younger than D'oro was now. How tragic it must have been for her.

D'oro found nothing of further interest until May 16 of the following year. "Silver Queen Resumes Shipment of Ore to the Selby Smelter." The short article told that Jim Gregg, partner in the Silver Queen Mine, had found a new vein that appeared to be as rich as the pocket he and Franklin Baxter found in March of the previous year, and shipment of ore to the Selby, California, smelter had resumed.

A week later a small item near the bottom of the front page announced, "Jim Gregg Claims Bride." It told only that popular Mariposa bachelor Jim Gregg married Miss Sally Anderson of Las Vegas in a civil ceremony, and that the newlyweds would make their home in Mariposa.

In contrast the spot reserved for the town's important social events in the June 27 *Gazette* told of the wedding of Miss Ann Baxter to Clay Nalton of Coulterville, an elaborate event in a local church.

After that, D'oro found that most Mariposa social events contained the names of Clay and Ann Nalton and Jim and Sally Gregg. Wondering that neither her father nor Annie had mentioned a friendship with the other, D'oro was preparing to return the large bound volume to the attendant when a headline caught her with a force that was almost physical: "Clay Nalton Killed in Silver Queen Cave-In—Jim Gregg Held for Murder."

With staring, unbelieving eyes D'oro read the details. Clay Nalton had been working in the shaft of the Silver Queen and had signaled to his partner, Jim Gregg, to start the hoist. Halfway down, the cable snapped, flinging the broken cable and ore bucket against the opposite wall of the shaft, causing a massive landslide. Rescue workers were unable to unblock the shaft to recover the body. Investigation revealed that the hoist cable had been cut, and Gregg was charged with the murder of his partner. The paper was dated April 17, 1957.

The letters on the page in front of her wriggled and squirmed like black snakes. D'oro gripped the table to steady herself.

It simply couldn't be true! Her father was so kind, so understanding with other people. The idea of him hurting or killing anyone was unthinkable. Hastily D'oro turned to the next issue, looking for an explanation of what must have been an error. There was a short account of the memorial service at the Silver Queen Mine for Clay Nalton, and a list of survivors: Ann Baxter Nalton and Clay's four brothers in Coulterville. There was no mention of the cause of death.

D'oro quickly turned to the following week's paper but found no mention of the Silver Queen or anyone associated with it. It was as if the hateful story had not been printed. Finally in the May 15 issue she found her father's name again with the announcement of the birth of a baby girl to Jim and Sally Gregg. Had her father been in jail, charged with murder, when she was born? The whole thing was preposterous!

Two issues later there was a brief announcement: "Gregg trial to begin tomorrow. Superior Court Judge Joseph Brimmer will preside." The district attorney was named, as was the lawyer representing her father.

A single column in the upper left of the next week's front page finished the story. GREGG VERDICT IN. "A jury of nine men and three women yesterday acquitted Jim Gregg of charges of murdering his partner, Clay Nalton. The verdict of not guilty was returned at 12:30 P.M. after fifty minutes of deliberation following the three-day trial. More than twenty witnesses testified during the hearing, which was presided over by Judge Brimmer." The list of prosecution witnesses was short: the deputy sheriff who investigated the accident, and a number of men who had witnessed a violent quarrel between Nalton and Gregg at the Bootstompers' Dance. The list of defense witnesses was much longer, but the only name D'oro recognized was Ann Nalton. Her father had testified in his own behalf. The account was full of the names of everyone who had participated in the trial in any capacity, but none of the facts and arguments. In a small-town newspaper it seemed names were the news.

D'oro stared blankly at the paper for a long time, two unanswered questions whirling in her mind: What had actually happened at the Silver

Queen? Why had her father fled to Mexico after being acquitted?

Finally her legs felt steady enough for her to get up, return the large volume to the counter, and slip quietly out the door. The hallway was a haze, as were the display cases in the entryway. A sign above a corner stairway she hadn't noticed when she came in pushed its way into her consciousness: SUPERIOR COURTROOM. Drawn as if by a magnet, she climbed the narrow angled stairs to the room where her father had stood trial twenty-six years before.

The courtroom had a Spartan atmosphere, little changed in its hundred-year use. The white-washed pine plank walls were unadorned except for a pair of silver electrified kerosene lamps with saucerlike reflectors mounted behind the judge's desk, and an American flag that stood beside it. The windows were bare with white pull-down shades. The judge's desk and other furniture were golden oak, solid and well worn.

D'oro huddled on one of the narrow spectators' benches and stared at the jury box, feeling the tragic drama of the day when her father had sat before his friends and neighbors, accused of murdering his partner, Annie's husband. She tried to picture her father there and Annie. What had they looked like? How had they felt? And Sally with a new baby just a few weeks old—had she been there? Somehow D'oro thought not. There had been no mention of her in the newspaper account. D'oro knew her father would not have wanted the outcome of his trial to have rested on the emotional appeal of his wife and baby.

There she stood twenty-six years later, discovering at least part of the story everyone involved seemed to have conspired to keep from her. She felt like Pandora, who pried into a box and allowed all the troubles of the world to escape. Tears streaming down her face, D'oro stumbled down the narrow stairs and out into the driving rain that had been threatening since early morning.

Chapter Six

When Annie finally convinced her lawyer and longtime friend that she could not be dissuaded from her intended course of action, drawing the deed took only a few minutes. It was twenty minutes until four when she returned to the library. She was surprised to find that D'oro was not there. Annie described D'oro to Mrs. Jenkins, the librarian, and asked if she had noticed when she left and if she had indicated where she might be going.

"Yes, the young lady left about forty-five minutes ago. She expressed interest in one of the ore specimens in the safe. When she said it was not from the original gold rush, I told her that we didn't have any books on later finds. I suggested she might find the information in back issues of the *Mariposa Gazette* in the county clerk's office."

"Thank you, Mrs. Jenkins." Annie crossed the room with quick purposeful steps, pausing a moment to scowl at the safe. It had been a long time since she had really looked at the gleaming quartz and silver specimen that was a token of the tragedy that still clouded her life. How much did D'oro know about the accident that had closed the Silver Queen? Annie cursed the cowardice and pride that had kept her from talking about it when D'oro raised questions.

A driving rain had begun to pelt against the overhanging roof, but Annie ignored it as she dashed to her car and spun the powerful Porsche up the hill and parked in front of the courthouse. D'oro was coming out of the building. She walked as if she were in a trance. Annie recalled the similar feeling that the world had fallen away beneath her feet as she walked out of that same door twenty-six years ago after Jim's trial.

Jim hadn't told his daughter about it! Annie could tell by the tears that streamed down D'oro's face to be washed away in the drenching rain to which she seemed oblivious. What an awful way to learn about the whole sorry mess—to read it in the newspaper, even ones that old. Annie got out of the car and sprinted up the walk to put her arm protectively around D'oro's hunched shoulders.

"He didn't tell me...you didn't tell me," D'oro sobbed.

"I know, and we were both wrong. He wanted to protect you. I haven't any excuse." Annie guided her to the car and opened the door.

Wordlessly D'oro climbed in, dripping rivulets of water around her. Annie longed to put her arms around the other woman and comfort her. She was so young, so vulnerable. There was nothing she could say that would ease the pain. It was still too new and raw. Why hadn't she told her when D'oro asked if she knew her father? Annie thought with deep remorse. How could you tell someone who adored her father that he had been accused of murder? He had been acquitted, of course, but there had still been unanswered questions. Had she really been sure? Scenes she had blocked from her mind for many years began flooding back as she drove the interminable distance to the ranch.

Clay was drunk and in an ugly mood when he staggered home that Friday night. Five days had passed since she had seen him, and she was beginning to hope that he had left for good.

"Why don't you go back to your floozie? I don't want you around," she told him when he began to cover her with drunken slobbery kisses. He reeked of whiskey and perspiration and an odd dank smell, as if he had been sleeping in someone's root cellar.

Clay laughed like the joke was on her. "Tonight I want you. Tomorrow I'll go back to my other love. But don't think you're going to get rid of me so easy."

She managed to get away from him and seek refuge in her locked room. In the end Clay broke down the door. His assault on her was vicious and brutal—not the cat-and-mouse game that had seemed to amuse him before. When he finally collapsed into a drunken stupor, she managed to escape to an empty room in the bunkhouse to cry out her pain and humiliation. She knew then she would divorce Clay. If necessary, she would hire guards to protect her and the ranch. No man could treat Ann Baxter the way he had treated her.

Early in the morning she took one of the horses and rode out to watch from a distant hill until Clay left the ranch. Then she gathered up all of his things and put them in a box and took the box to the woodshed. She was surprised how little there was. She did not go to see her lawyer that day, as bruises were beginning to show on her face that could not be covered.

Toward evening she heard Jim's car driving down the valley. Never had she needed him so desperately, but she didn't want him to see her like that. It was too late. There were lights on in the house, and her own car stood in the drive. He did not go to the front door. As he had from long habit he walked around to the back and across the patio, where he saw her through the kitchen window.

He took one look at her and asked, "Did Clay do that to you?"

With tears streaming down her cheeks she silently nodded.

"I'll kill him," he said quietly.

"No, Jim—he isn't worth it. I'll file for divorce as soon as I'm presentable to go into town. He hadn't been home for days. He's shacking up with some tramp somewhere. That new wrangler, Buck, will be back Monday, and I'll hire another man." It started as a broken speech but gained strength as she went along.

"You have more courage than any woman I've ever known." He put his arms around her gently and eased her head against his chest to cry it out. "What have I done to you, little one?" he asked, stroking her hair as he had done when she was eighteen and her parents had been killed.

When she was calm, Jim went into town to get new locks for the doors. He took the box of Clay's belongings with him and he found Clay at the Bootstompers' Dance. That was when the fight took place that several witnesses reported at the trial. One quoted him as saying, "If you ever go near her again, I'll kill you." It was assumed Jim was speaking of his wife, Sally. There was no suspicion that Clay was having an affair with Sally at that critical time, because Sally was in Los Angeles with her sister to be near specialists when the baby arrived. There had been complications.

Jim returned and changed the locks, then Annie fixed him dinner, the first food she had eaten in twenty-four hours. Afterward they sat quietly on the big leather couch until finally she fell asleep with her head on his shoulder. He picked her up as if she were a child and carried her to the guest room—the room that became D'oro's. With gentle hands he undressed her, probing, soothing the bruises. Finally he covered her with a sheet and lay down beside her. She snuggled against him, absorbing his strength and his protection. Gently he made love to her with restraint and sensitivity. When she again found sleep in his arms, she was free of the terror and deep psychic wounds Clay had inflicted on her.

When Annie awoke in the morning, Jim had already left for Los Angeles to keep his appointment with Sally. By midafternoon a big quiet man appeared at the ranch, telling her he had heard she was looking for a hired hand. She knew Jim had sent him. On Monday the accident happened at the Silver Queen. Clay was dead, and Jim was accused of his murder.

How could she have told Jim's daughter of the tragedy without raising more questions than she could answer? Annie glanced at the young woman sitting beside her as immobile as if she were made of ice and slowly melting away into the small pools of water around her on the seat and on the floor.

By the time they arrived at the ranch, Annie had found the control of her emotions that she had so carefully built for over twenty years. "Better go get dried off and warmed up. Then I think we should talk."

D'oro showered and changed. She had little fear of catching cold, as it was a warm day and she was not subject to illness. She toweled her hair as dry as possible, slipped on a warm robe, and went to find Annie, who was in the kitchen pouring steaming mugs of hot chocolate spiced with cinnamon, the way Maria had made it for D'oro when she was a little girl.

D'oro wrapped her hands around the warm mug to keep them from trembling as she asked, "My father was a partner with you and your— family in the Silver Queen?"

"Yes. Jim was my partner, my friend, my business adviser, and my source of strength when my parents were killed." She did not mention the other time that was so much on her mind when Jim had provided the strength she needed.

D'oro thought she detected a hint in the older woman's voice that Annie had been in love with her father. The thought that Nalton might have been killed as part of a love triangle seemed preposterous when people like Annie and her father were involved. Both of them were too compassionate, too caring to take their happiness at someone else's expense, even though D'oro had never felt that her father was in love with Sally.

"Did he kill him?" she asked in a voice so low, it was barely audible. She could not bring herself to say "Did my father kill your husband?"

"The jury didn't think so. He was acquitted." Annie said it as if it were a mantra she had repeated over and over to herself throughout the years.

"After he was found not guilty, why did he run away to Mexico?" D'oro haltingly asked the final hateful question and immediately felt pangs of disloyalty for having asked.

"Running away, as you call it, was not easy for Jim. We talked about it for hours the day he was acquitted." Closing her eyes, Annie could still see the sorrow etched on his handsome face. It was the last time she had seen or heard from him. Again she seemed to be repeating often recited words. "You and Sally were so vulnerable. You see, Clay—" She stopped then as if it had been a long time since she had said the name. "Clay had four brothers in Coulterville, a mean, rough bunch who would stop at nothing if they felt a wrong had been done one of them, and they set their minds on revenge."

D'oro recalled what the old miner in Coulterville had said about the Nalton brothers, even about the expectation that they would have raised hell down in Mariposa after Clay's death.

"You testified for my father. Weren't you in danger, too?"

"No. If there was one thing stronger than the Naltons' drive for vengeance, it was their greed. I was their only chance to recover Clay's share of the Silver Queen." She didn't mention that the big quiet hired hand had stayed on at the ranch for the next six months, doing whatever odd jobs could be found to occupy his time and staying very much to himself.

"But the Naltons didn't get any part of the Silver Queen?"

"Funny thing, they didn't even try very hard. They sent a claim through a shyster lawyer. My lawyer rejected it, and I never heard any more from them. Of course, the shaft was pretty badly damaged. It would have taken a lot of work to get it back in operation. The Naltons didn't even show up to protest when my lawyer asked the court to declare Clay legally dead a couple of years ago when I sold Bret the Heartbreaker Mine. Clay's body was never recovered."

D'oro wondered how much of the story of the Silver Queen Bret knew and if he had made the connection between her and her father. She wondered what effect such knowledge might have on their relationship. What relationship? she mocked herself, recalling that he was even then off somewhere with his Candy. To him, D'oro was just an employee whose family connections shouldn't matter so long as she did her job. But she had failed at that, too. What a mess it had all turned out to be. She wished she had never gone to Mariposa, but it was a mistake that would soon be corrected, she was convinced.

Thinking of the tragedy of so many years ago that still cast its shadow today, D'oro asked, "Was my father in jail when I was born?"

"No. Jim was well liked and highly respected in Mariposa. He was released on bond, except during the trial." And he had been in a self-imposed prison ever since, Annie thought bitterly.

Chapter Seven

The rain sheeting against the windows isolating them from the rest of the world seemed an appropriate background for Annie's account of the grim events that had sent Jim Gregg into exile in Mexico. During the night the rain beating on the roof provided a hypnotic rhythm bringing restless sleep. The morning was gray and dreary, but the rain had finally stopped. By the time D'oro was dressed, Annie was setting a light tempting breakfast on the table. Both women made a pretense of eating to encourage the other. The tragedy of the Silver Queen, which had altered the course of both their lives, had formed a special bond between them, but that morning they talked only about the weekend racing meet at Santa Anita in which Annie had entered one of her young quarter horses.

The day brightened as D'oro drove to the mine. Thor was in a playful mood when he greeted her arrival, so she raced him back to the laboratory. As she rounded the corner of the hoist house she was startled to see that the laboratory door was open. Bret was standing at the workbench, staring at the unresponsive flask of murky liquid and zinc pellets.

"Didn't work, did it?" he said simply without derision or show of emotion.

"No," she answered, trying to keep her voice as free of emotion as his was.

"Didn't work for me, either."

"It did work in Juan's laboratory. I've done it lots of times," she said defensively.

"But the formula differs for different silver ores?"

"Yes. That's why I checked each mineral contained in the ore separately to determine its effect on the solution."

"What'll you do now?"

"Start over and check each element again—find out what I missed."

He smiled at her then, apparently pleased by her persistence. "Before you do, would you like to go down in the tunnel to see the ore in its natural state? It might give you a clue?"

D'oro's spirits soared. She had wanted to go down in the mine to see where Bret spent his time since the day she had first watched his ingenious system for bringing ore to the surface and dumping it automatically.

"I'd love to," she answered with enthusiasm, then hesitated. 'But the answer to the problem isn't down in the tunnel, it's here in the laboratory—something I've overlooked, a mistake I made somewhere."

"Well, come on, anyway, maybe you'll get

some inspiration down there." Then his voice became doubtful. "You do know what you're letting yourself in for? It's two hundred feet down to the level where I'm working. That's like climbing to the top of a twenty-story building, no elevator."

"Or climbing our Temple of the Sun. I wouldn't want to do it twice a day the way you do, but I'm sure I can make it one time," she said eagerly.

"Do you happen to have a jacket in your car? The temperature that deep in the earth stays an even sixty-two degrees."

She nodded.

"On second thought, maybe we should wait until tomorrow. You really aren't dressed for exploring a mine," he said, eyeing her trim pale green slacks and open sandals.

"I have my acid day clothes in the car," D'oro suggested.

"Acid day?"

"Even in the heat of a Mexican summer Juan insisted I wear heavy clothes when I was decanting acids, so I keep some in the car for the times I have to decant acid from the large jugs into the laboratory containers. I have jeans, a moisture-proof jacket, socks, and sturdy shoes."

"How about gloves?"

"Those, too."

"Like a good girl scout, you're prepared," he teased.

D'oro was glad something she did pleased him, though she winced at his comparison as she remembered her hesitation when he kissed her during their Saturday ride.

"Prettiest miner I ever saw," he said as he helped her adjust her hard hat and miners' lamp and attach the battery to the belt of her jeans.

D'oro flushed in spite of herself. It seemed odd to be dressed for a winter expedition there in the warm California sunshine.

The double doors that secured the entrance to the shaft were already open when she climbed the three steps to the portal entrance and looked from the bright sunlight into the gloom of the seemingly bottomless shaft. Bret led the way as they started to descend the ladder, its bottom lost in a pit of darkness. The portal area resembled a wooden-sided elevator shaft. D'oro was surprised to find the first ladder was no longer than one that would reach from the floor to the hayloft of a tall barn. Then they were standing on a wooden platform. A second ladder protruded through a manhole in the platform.

"I thought it would be all one long ladder," she said.

"No. A mine is dug in a series of levels. The upper platforms give extra strength and provide a working area when repairs are necessary. Lower platforms mark the various levels where drifts were run in search of the vein. Besides, if you lose your footing on the ladder, you only fall one stage, not the full length of the shaft."

From the half-joking tone of his voice D'oro was not sure how serious he was about the last comment. It was hard to imagine the agile man who was descending with such ease ever falling off a ladder.

Below the second platform the construction of the shaft changed. It became solid rock braced with timbers holding the track for the ore bucket, securing the ladder in place, and supporting crumbly sections of the wall. Her eyes had become accustomed to the gloom, which had the quality of early twilight. It was noticeably cooler, and she was surprised to find a fresh breeze blowing up the shaft.

D'oro was thoroughly enjoying herself, except for the nagging feeling that being shown the mine was like a consolation given a child who has had a disappointment, timed to be a peace offering after the previous day's encounter with Candy.

"Shall we take a breather?" he asked at the eighth level.

"I'm not tired, but I have been noticing some changes in the shaft I wondered about."

"You mean the moisture on the walls and the occasional sound of dripping water?"

"Yes. It's so quiet down here, you seem to hear the slightest sound."

"The silence is one of the things a miner finds good about his work. The water is just ground seepage. We'll be below it in another level or two."

At the tenth level an inky black hole opened up beside them.

"There was some silver outcropping on the wall of the shaft here, so I ran a short drift at this level, but it proved to be only isolated rocks not connected with the main vein, so I went on down."

It had become quite dark, and their miners'

lamps were showing full beams when Bret announced, "Welcome to the treasure house."

Laughing, D'oro turned halfway to face him as her foot sought the floor of the shaft, but she found herself dangling in space, unable to find anything solid on which to place her extended foot. Bret's strong hands reached out to lift her from the ladder and pull her close against his broad powerful shoulders.

D'oro felt like Alice tumbling down the rabbit hole into Wonderland. The light was soft and eerie. Their elongated shadow cast by Bret's miners' lamp flickered across the dust-gray walls. Her heart pounded and her pulse raced. She felt lightheaded, almost dizzy, but she knew the sensation was not caused by the long climb or the missed step. She looked up at the outline of Bret's rugged handsome face bending toward her with the light shining from his forehead like an ancient cyclops. His lamp flashed across her closed eyelids as his lips lightly brushed her temple and then found her waiting lips. That time as his mouth crushed hers there were words of love, not from him but from her own heart, whose staccato beat said all too clearly, *te quiero,* "I love you." Her soft full lips invited, responded to his kiss.

Bret's arms tightened around her, pulling her close against him, but with heavy jackets and gloves on it felt like they were bear cubs hugging. His hand went to the zipper of her jacket, hesitated, and stopped. With the flush of desire pounding in her veins, she was not even aware that the air around them was cold. Bret laughed huskily and set her on her feet, saying, "Caught you on my sneak-thief step."

"Your sneak-thief step?" she questioned, trying desperately to conceal the frustration and confusion she felt.

"Yes. Old houses were built with one step longer than the rest so that a thief in the night would stumble and be heard by the household. In my case I must confess it was pure laziness. I built the last step where I needed it for my own long legs. I should have warned you."

D'oro could only laugh politely at his joke as she taunted herself for being a fool to long for a man who obviously saved his love for someone else. At least she was certain the high-heeled, silk-stockinged Candy had never been brought down in the mine; small consolation to her wounded pride.

Bret readjusted the battery for D'oro's light, which had gone out when she tripped. He gave the switch a tap, and the dancing beam of her head-lamp joined his, playing tag against the far wall. Bret seemed to be making a game of it, attempting to restore the mood of lighthearted adventure with which they had started.

"This is the drift I'm working," he said, leading her toward an inky black hole. "Keep your head ducked, as the top of the tunnel is uneven."

The air was fresh but smelled earthy and a little musty as she followed him into the darkness. Her lamp outlined his lean athletic legs and hips. When they had gone about twenty feet, he turned back to her and turned off his light.

"Turn around and turn off your light, then look back toward the shaft."

She did as he told her. A faint light the intensity of a candle without the flicker showed at the end of the coal-black tunnel in which they were standing. It was an awesome sight, one that made her glad for the presence of the powerful man standing beside her. Again his light pierced the enveloping blackness and he led the way another short distance until the light was reflected back from a solid rock wall. A drill similar to those she had seen used for breaking pavement lay at the base of the wall.

"This is how I drill my dynamite holes," he said, picking up the drill and bracing it against his shoulder. As he pulled the trigger the silence was broken by the rat-tat-tat of the drill against solid rock. "Depending on the structure of the rock, I usually place ten to twelve charges per shot."

"And then count them when you are on the surface to be sure they all go off?" she asked, recalling her first day at the laboratory, when he stood by the door and counted the separate rumblings.

"That's right. And this is the skimmer that takes the ore to the bucket," he said, pointing to a square of metal suspended by a pulley wheel from a single track she had noticed running along the wall about waist high.

D'oro was surprised to find that the automated ore-dumping system she had watched on the surface had the preliminary underground step. She felt stupid not to have realized that the ore bucket, which climbed up and down the tracks in the shaft, could not go into the drift for ore. She knew enough about mining to recognize the skill of the engineer beside her who had designed the system she had seen in its entirety. "Must be an easier way to make a living—or a fortune," she said, teasing.

"That's what I tell myself frequently, but there's a great deal of satisfaction to mining when it gets in your blood. Like hunting, there's the thrill of the chase, the challenge of finding a hidden treasure. For the man who owns his own mine, it means independence. There's the wonderful silence until I break it myself with some activity. Mainly I think it's the struggle, yet the harmony with one of the elemental forces of nature." He stopped and looked embarrassed to have revealed so much of his inner feelings.

"I think my father too loved mining when he did it the way you are, but there's not much of that satisfaction in being part of a big operation like he is now. He seldom talks about his early experiences."

A smile abruptly vanished from Bret's eyes, a muscle rippled along his firm jaw, and he answered brusquely, "This isn't a sight-seeing trip, as I warned you. Here is the vein we're working with."

Puzzled as to what had caused his abrupt change of attitude, D'oro stepped close to the end of the drift and examined the two-foot ribbon of white quartz shining with square mirrorlike pieces of iron pyrites, sometimes called fool's gold. He produced a miners' lens from a thong around his neck. Through it she could see the dark streaks and tiny beads of silver, a few scattered flecks of gold, occasional colorful tracings of copper, but nothing she had not found in the pieces of crushed ore in the laboratory. Then she examined the material surrounding the vein—gray decomposed granite mixed with a whitish clay, occasional streaks of rust from iron, but nothing that hadn't shown up in the spectrograph. She removed her right glove and ran her fingers speculatively over the vein, noting the tight hard crystalline surface of the quartz, the sharply angled edges of the pyrite, and the crumbly, gritty feeling of decomposed granite. Slowly she shook her head.

"Maybe it's time to try some of that inspiration I mentioned." Bret sat down on the floor of the tunnel, stretched his long legs out in front of him, and rested his back against the wall. He motioned her down beside him. "This is where I solve my toughest problems," he said, turning out his lamp and indicating that she should do the same.

D'oro found the floor to be moist but not saturated. She had experienced such total darkness only once before when she had visited mineral caverns and the guide had turned out the lights. She could sense the elemental power Bret spoke of, the solid rock beneath her and behind her shoulders, the total absence of light and sound. She felt the tension of her muscles relax and her mind clear. There was an otherworld quality to the silent stygian darkness.

Bret's fingers slipped under her gloveless hand, cradling it from the harshness of the rock floor. His long powerful fingers enclosed hers as if she were a novice being led by a reassuring hand into a mystic rite. She allowed her subconscious to take command as she experienced the ethereal feeling that time and place had vanished with the light, leaving a unity with the primeval forces in Bret and his mine. As her ears adapted to the absence of the usual sounds of the earth, D'oro could hear Bret's deep rhythmic breathing. Automatically her breathing paced itself to his, creating a deeper feeling of harmony between them. There in Bret's special world, with only his fingers touching hers, she felt the communication of unspoken words, an intimacy of spirit beyond the most passionate kiss.

His thumb began to stroke the back of her hand in lazy sensuous circles, arousing an eagerness in the rest of her body to feel the caress of his hands. Since the day she arrived she had dreamed of being accepted into the world of Bret's work. Once she was there at least for a brief moment, she knew she wanted more. She wanted to share every part of his life—she wanted him.

All of her senses were so concentrated on Bret's sitting beside her in the darkness, she almost screamed when a small flicker of flame appeared in the blackness and began to move toward them.

"Your eyes are pools of liquid silver." His voice had a soft, deep resonance as if it came from the rocks themselves.

"I think they melted when you lit that match. That was quite a trick with one hand." She laughed unsteadily.

"Learned it from an old miner. It brings me back to reality." His lips burned a kiss into the palm of her hand, more searing than any match might have been. He helped her to her feet. D'oro knew those moments of darkness in the mine had been a very special kind of sharing that she would never forget. She wondered if it had been special for him, too.

Bret was preoccupied as they began the long climb to the surface. He seemed to have a new sense of purpose about his movements, as if he had reached a decision sitting beside her in the dark tunnel.

Back in the laboratory he helped her remove her miners' hat and jacket.

"I have business in town the next couple of days," he said in a manner that told her he was already beginning to put his decision into operation. "I should be finished by Friday morning. Would you like to take that day off and drive up to Yosemite? The weekend rain should have started a good flow over the falls again."

"I'd love to," she answered, her spirits soaring at the prospect of a pleasure trip with Bret without the intrusion of mining business. Her hopes were dashed when he turned abruptly and strode purposefully from the laboratory, as if he had checked off one item in the plan he had decided on.

Dejectedly she turned her attention to the flask that contained the mute evidence of the failure of her work. She picked up the spectrographic report, the piece of modern technology that made her work possible. That single sheet of paper listed fifty-three minerals from aluminum to zirconium and indicated the percentage of those found in a given ore sample as determined by the wavelength of each mineral arranged in a spectrum.

D'oro had worked so carefully the first time, analyzing each of the eighteen marked items. For many reasons she wanted desperately for the process to work. First she had been determined to show Bret she could make the formula work. It would be her contribution tò his dream of starting a mining revival for Mariposa. She had been so certain of the results when she started, but something was wrong. It would take her two days to recheck each element. She could be ready to try again by Thursday afternoon. Bret had invited her to go to Yosemite on Friday. Suddenly the two timetables meshed. He knew the time it would take her to redo the experiment. He expected her to fail again! That was the conclusion he had reached as they sat in the darkness of the tunnel. He had begun already to follow whatever course of action he had decided her failure would make necessary. The trip to Yosemite was intended to soften the blow of a second failure, and at the same time be a farewell gesture to conclude her work for him. D'oro found more pain in the thought of leaving Mariposa and never seeing Bret again than she had found in all of the other disappointments and problems she had encountered since going there. She had to prove Bret wrong about her failing again.

Grimly she set to work doing the job in which

she had always found so much satisfaction. With discipline she had learned from Juan Rodriguez during long patient years, she concentrated her full attention on the work at hand until lengthening shadows falling across her workbench told her she had worked an hour beyond her usual quitting time. As she locked up the laboratory D'oro noticed that Bret's pickup had not returned.

With her thoughts still mulling over the work of the day, she was startled by the persistent ringing of a bell. She followed the sound into the hoist house and was amused to find that the ringing was a telephone mounted on the wall beside the door. It was certainly not a busy line. In the time D'oro had been at the Heartbreaker she had never heard it ring before. She picked up the receiver, but before she could say anything she was greeted by "Hello, darling," in Candy's sultry affected manner.

"Heartbreaker Mine," D'oro responded in the most businesslike tone she could command. The long pause that followed her statement reminded D'oro of the comedy routine "If a woman answers, hang up."

"May I speak to Bret, please?" It was a command, not a question, and the please was purely perfunctory.

"Bret isn't here. May I take a message?" answered D'oro, still trying for office-routine efficiency.

"No, thank you. I'll call back later," Candy snapped and hung up with a sharp click.

D'oro's amused smile quickly faded when she

realized the implication of Candy's words. It was apparent she was familiar with Bret's routine and regularly called him at that time of day, anticipating he would be the one answering when she heard the receiver lifted. Was Candy calling to arrange another tryst? Was that Bret's business in town?

D'oro slammed the door of the hoist house behind her as she would be slamming the door on that brief interlude in her life after the trip to Yosemite with Bret, after which would be the difficult part—trying to forget him. As if to show that he was on her side, Thor trotted out from the shadow of the trailer to escort her to her car before returning to his self-appointed guard duties.

It was only when the ranch house was in sight that the memory of past sorrows rushed back to add to the problems of the present. As she drove into the yard D'oro regarded the sprawling Spanish hacienda with new appreciation. Each of its handcrafted features had been lovingly created by a workman to whom it meant opportunity during the bleak days of the jobless Depression. She felt sure it was no coincidence that many of its details had been duplicated in her own home in Zacatecas.

Her heels rang hollowly on the red tile floor, echoing her solitary presence in the house and reaffirming Annie's absence at a racing meet in which one of her young quarter horses was entered. D'oro rubbed absently at the back of her neck where signs of tension were beginning to appear. It had been a very long day. She would not admit that Bret's absence made it seem longer.

Though the sun was disappearing behind the mountain, she headed directly for the barn. Since her childhood a brisk ride on her favorite horse had been the antidote for trouble or loneliness. Apparently busy tending to the extra duties required by Annie's absence, Rattlesnake was nowhere in sight. D'oro quickly saddled Bonanza and headed across the west pasture beyond which the purple mountain was crested by a rim of silver from the setting sun. The air was fresh and a gentle breeze tugged at her hair. The spirited horse responded to her every motion, his flawless rhythm soothing away the worries and tensions of the day.

The first stars were faintly twinkling in the sky when D'oro reluctantly turned back to the ranch. Rattlesnake was busying himself in the corral when she returned, waiting for her, she was sure. Like her father waiting for her to return from a date, she thought with amusement.

"Didn't expect you to ride this evenin' when you was so late gettin' home from work," he said apologetically.

"Thought I'd take a little run to blow the dust devils out of my mind. It's been a bad day," she said as she handed Bonanza's reins over to his outstretched hand.

"Didn't stop to eat any dinner," he accused.

"No, and I'll bet you haven't eaten, either."

The twisted grin that wrought such a change in his craggy face acknowledged that he had not.

"Come in when you have finished cooling

down Bonanza, and we'll see what we can rustle up," she invited.

When D'oro went to inspect the refrigerator, she found all the ingredients for a Mexican dinner neatly arranged together on one shelf. D'oro silently acknowledged Lupe's gesture of caring as she removed a stack of freshly made tortillas, ground beef, bright red chilies, grated yellow cheese, and black olives—all for enchiladas. There was a ripe avocado for guacamole salad and pre-cooked beans for refrying.

The enchiladas were already in the oven when Rattlesnake joined her in the kitchen. He sniffed appreciatively at the spicy aroma and settled with pleasure in one of the chairs at the table she was spreading with a red plaid tablecloth.

D'oro had never cooked dinner for a more appreciative guest. She was glad she had cooked ample quantities as she watched in amazement the quantity of food the small man managed to eat.

"Best Mexican chow I've tasted since I left Texas," he said as he scraped up the last of the frijoles.

"Have you worked here long?" D'oro asked.

"Since Annie's pa built the ranch. I was just a kid driftin' around lookin' for work. He started me breakin' mustangs for saddle horses for the ranches hereabout."

"And you've been here ever since?"

"'Cept for a couple of years I went back to Texas after I had a fight with Clay Nalton. Only real fight I ever had, and I whipped him, too."

The small man's eyes twinkled as he leaned his chair back against the wall and warmed to his tale.

"Guess I was just so plumb mad I forgot how much bigger 'n me he was. He was showin' off on one of the mustangs that wasn't quite broke when it threw him. He picked up a broken-off fence post and went after that horse, an' I went after him—hit him low, down around the knees. The post flew one way and him the other. I was on top of him 'fore he hit the ground, and kept swingin' away until he had to say he'd had enough."

"Was that after he and Annie were married?"

"Yep. 'Bout a year after."

"Did he fire you?"

"No. That wasn't Clay Nalton's way. Real sneaky mean he was, and always set on gettin' even. Figured I didn't hanker to spend my days lookin' out for a fellow waitin' to bushwhack me, so I went back to Texas."

"Why did you come back?"

"Friend sent me a clippin' about the accident."

"Did you know my father?" she asked hesitantly, not certain that she wanted to probe farther into the past, but unable to leave the questions unanswered.

"Jim Gregg," he acknowledged. "I remember the day he came drivin' in here. Handsome young feller. Kinda' puts me in mind of your friend owns the big silver stallion."

His comparison amused and pleased her. It meant she wasn't just a romantic schoolgirl imagining similarities between her father and the man she loved.

Encouraged by her smile, he continued. "Spring of '52 it was. Gregg was a mining engineer fresh outa college, but he wasn't a know-it-all like some of 'em. Baxter took a likin' to him right away. Gave him a job at the Silver Queen. Made him a partner when Gregg made the big strike in '53."

"Did he live here at the ranch?"

"No. Baxter had an old cabin over by the mine 'fore he built the ranch. Gregg fixed that up real comfortable. He used to come here often for dinner, though. Mrs. Baxter, she liked him, too, and Annie was a real caution. Back then she was a little skinny gal. Wore her hair in pigtails and was brown as an Indian. She'd rather be out bustin' a bronc than in the house helpin' her ma. When Gregg got to comin' round for dinner, you wouldn't know it was the same girl, hair all brushed out real wavy and a pretty dress on. Don't think she ever owned a dress before, except maybe for school. He didn't have no family and he treated her just like his kid sister. He used to take her and her friends to the square dances on Saturday night at the Bootstompers' Hall. Her pa wouldn't let her go with one of the other kids drivin'."

D'oro poured them both another cup of coffee. A warm glow seeped through her as she listened to the old cowboy's words. That was the first account she had heard of the happy part of her father's years in Mariposa.

After a long drink of the steaming brew, Rattlesnake resumed his story. "When her folks were killed in a car accident, Gregg really took on the job of big brother. The find at the Silver Queen was just a rich pocket, not a vein, and it began to peter out. Money was kinda' scarce around here after that. Annie talked about sellin' the ranch, but he wouldn't hear of it. He said it was her heritage and she should use her talent with horses to keep it. He even mortgaged the mine to buy the first quarter horses.''

"Did he help run the ranch?''

"No. He said everyone had to work out his own life. His was mining, hers was ranching. Don't know as she'd have made it that first year, though, if he hadn't found the real vein in the Silver Queen. I remember the night he found the Glory Hole. I'd just come in the back door when he came prancin' into the ranch house like a Thoroughbred into the winner's circle. He grabbed Annie round the waist and swung her clear off her feet. He put a shiny piece of ore in her hand. Looked like it was almost pure silver. 'This calls for a celebration,' he shouted. 'Where would you like to go? Las Vegas, San Francisco, Los Angeles, or maybe on down into Mexico?''' Rattlesnake paused for another gulp of coffee.

"I was still in the kitchen. They couldn't see me, but I could see them in the big silver-framed mirror that hangs over the sideboard. Well, Annie looks up at him real pert like and says, 'Will you make love to me if we go to Mexico?' Jim started to laugh, then stopped all of a sudden. He got a funny look on his face and the color began to come up on the back of his neck. He wheeled around and stormed out of here like a whirlwind that's suddenly changed course. Annie just stood there stunned for a minute, then she kinda' crumpled down to the table and started bawlin'. I never was no good with a cryin' woman, so I patted her shoulder and told her, 'Never mind, he'll be back.'"

D'oro found it hard to imagine her father showing so much emotion—whether excitement or anger. Careful control was so much a habit with him that the Mexicans sometimes called him El Frigido, the cool one, particularly if there was trouble or an accident at the mine.

"He came back, all right, 'bout a week later." Rattlesnake's voice interrupted her thoughts. "He'd been over in Las Vegas celebratin' like any miner with a lucky strike—drinkin' and gamblin'. Brought this little gal back with him, cute as a brand-new colt and about as helpless. They'd been married a couple of days."

D'oro listened to his words as if he were talking about strangers instead of her parents. It was ironic that even though the other woman had been her mother—the glamorous show girl who had married her father—D'oro felt a closer identity with Annie in that long-ago triangle. Rattlesnake's story just didn't fit her father as she had known him. He drank very little and never gambled, not even in the friendly poker games the company officers sometimes held. She could almost hear her father saying "A man who hasn't the sense to hold on to good luck when it comes his way hasn't any business gambling."

Rattlesnake cleared his throat and began again,

determined to finish the story he had begun. "Well, it wasn't long after that Annie married Clay Nalton. He was a handsome devil, and he could sure turn on the charm when there was somethin' he wanted—and he wanted Miss Annie, or her pa's half of the Silver Queen, I never could figure out which. Anyhow, he was a hard worker, and with him and Gregg workin' the mine together it began to pay off big. That's about the time me and Nalton had the fight and I left."

"But you came back after the accident?"

"Figured Annie would be needin' me then."

"Were you here during the trial?"

"No. I had to settle up my business down in Texas. It was all over, and your pa and Miss Sally were gone when I got back."

"Did Annie tell you about the accident?"

"Nope. She never mentioned the mine to me, an' I never asked. We just set to work buildin' up the ranch."

They sat in silence for several minutes, each aware of the way that long-ago tragedy still shadowed their lives. Rattlesnake said good night, but D'oro dawdled over cleaning up the kitchen. She was in no hurry to retire to her lonely room. When she finally made her way through the empty house, she paused beside the carved oak dining table, where Annie had cried out her heartbreak so many years before. She thought about Candy's phone call. Was history repeating itself? Was Bret taking a miners' holiday in Las Vegas with Candy?

Chapter Eight

With a skill born of long practice, Annie backed the horse trailer up to her customary stall at Santa Anita. Her handler, Hank Grubb, hurried out to meet her.

"How's his foot?" she asked anxiously.

"Just fine. Megatite should be really ready for this one," she answered as she helped Hank unfasten the tailgate so he could lead the gleaming black horse out.

"Excitin', ain't it, watchin' a two-year-old in his first big race?"

A month before, Annie would have agreed wholeheartedly that there was nothing more exciting than watching the inaugural of a horse she had raised herself. The race should have been particularly interesting after she had to scratch Megatite from the Fresno meet, but the events of the past week had reduced the race to a poor second in Annie's thoughts.

She spent the afternoon getting Megatite settled in, exercised, and rubbed down, then she drove the van to the motel near the track where she always stayed. She did not join other owners at the nearby lounge for cocktails and a late dinner as was her custom. A series of phone calls completed her business. She cleaned up, had an early dinner, and went to bed as soon as a parade of lackluster television programs had made her drowsy enough that there was some hope of sleep.

Sunrise found her at the track, stopwatch in hand, timing Megatite's workout. His best time was two tenths of a second better than any of them had anticipated, and her handler and her jockey, Mike, could barely mask their excitement. When the workout was over, Annie pressed her hands to her temples, lowered her pleasant husky voice, and said hesitantly, "Hank, I'm afraid I'm coming down with something. Can you and Mike handle things here at the track if I don't shake this and make it back before Saturday's race?"

Hank looked at her with alarm. For someone like Miss Annie not to be in the paddock before one of her horses ran, she had to be near death.

"Don't look so scared, Hank. Feels like the flu. You don't die of it, only wish you could for a short spell."

The handler shook his head in understanding. He and Annie had been friends for a good many years.

"Don't you worry about things here. Me and Mike can handle everything. You just take care of yourself. Let me know if there is anything I can do."

"Thanks, Hank. I knew I could count on you. I figure to just go to bed with some aspirin and a hot toddy and sleep it off." She had added the last in the hope of warding off solicitous calls to the motel about her.

"You okay to drive to the motel, or can I run you over?"

"I'll make it fine, Hank, but thanks just the same."

She drove the short distance to the motel and parked beside her unit, then called a cab. She picked up her still-packed suitcase and in minutes was on her way to Los Angeles International Airport. All the way to the airport she kept wondering if she was making a mistake, being a fool. She did not like the idea of meddling in other people's lives, but she could see the pattern of coming events as clearly as if she were a medium with genuine psychic powers. D'oro's work had been a failure. She was so like Jim in those things that Annie knew she had not been careless or made any mistakes. D'oro would go through the whole process again, but Annie was sure the results would be the same. She was pretty sure Bret agreed. Faced with the failure of her work, the distress of unearthing old skeletons in the closet, and with no encouragement from Bret, D'oro would simply leave Mariposa.

If the process worked, D'oro would continue her work in the lab until the mill was complete and in operation. She would have her chance with the man she loved. Annie did not doubt that D'oro loved Bret. D'oro was too much like Annie had been at that age for Annie to make light of her first real love. Though Annie sensed that Bret was attracted to the pretty, intelligent younger woman, she could not predict that he would return her love. Annie was determined that if there was anything she could do about it, D'oro would have her chance to make things right; that her whole life would not turn on misunderstandings and blind chance as her own had.

Annie arrived at the airport half an hour early for the flight to Guadalajara. The man at the newsstand seemed surprised when the attractive, expensively dressed woman asked him for a copy of the *Racing News*. He watched her covertly as she ran an experienced eye down the list of entries in whatever race interested her. He shrugged. You couldn't always tell a horse player by the cut of his clothes. He smiled at his own clever description as his eyes lingered on the woman's slender well-rounded hips, which moved with natural easy grace beneath close-fitting beige slacks. He saw her turn toward the bank of public telephones as if to make a call, then change her mind and hurry on toward the boarding gate. *Hope you've picked a winner, lady,* he thought, smiling to himself.

The delay was longer at the Guadalajara airport as Annie waited for the local flight to Zacatecas. The terminal was small and hot and overcrowded with large families greeting arriving members or people departing. Annie was beginning to think she was out of her mind in what she was doing, and she smiled to herself about all the cloak-and-dagger procedure. She hadn't wanted either Bret or D'oro to know what she was doing unless her errand was a success, but neither of them concerned themselves that much with her affairs. Time was running out, and her scheduled race so close to Los Angeles seemed to be the perfect opportunity. Once she was at Santa Anita she recognized that racing was the focal point of Hank's and Mike's lives. She didn't want to let them down by admitting it no longer was of hers. They simply wouldn't understand that she had something more important to do than the big race.

When the small plane finally departed for Zacatecas, it held only a handful of passengers. Almost as soon as the plane reached its cruising altitude it left the pleasant green of the valleys surrounding Guadalajara to fly over the dramatic lunar landscape of the Sierra Madre. It was less than an hour later that the small plane dropped between rugged peaks to the small landing field at Zacatecas. The terminal there could only be described as primitive, but at least there was a public telephone. There had been Mexican workers at the S/S and the mine for as long as Annie could remember, and she had learned Spanish almost as soon as she learned English. Though the service was slow, she had no difficulty getting the number of the Plata Nueva Mine or informing the switchboard operator there that she was calling the laboratory. She had considered calling Juan Rodriguez from Los Angeles or from Guadalajara, but she knew enough about innate Mexican courtesy to know it would be more difficult for him to refuse to see her if she was there in Zacatecas than it would be before she made the trip.

The voice that answered "Juan Rodriguez *aquí*," was soft but businesslike.

Deliberately Annie switched to English. "This is Senora Baxter from Mariposa, California. D'oro has been staying with me. She has a problem. May I come to the laboratory and discuss it with you?"

"D'oro isn't ill?" he asked with alarm.

"No. Her health is fine. It is her work I wish to discuss. When would it be convenient for me to come?" she pressed.

"We do not receive visitors at the laboratory," he said apologetically. "I'd be pleased to meet you at your hotel after work. Over dinner, perhaps."

Annie understood well the dual personality of the Mexican professional man. If he accepted an assignment at his place of work, he would perform the task responsibly and efficiently. If he met a woman socially, he would be gracious, flatter her outrageously, promise her anything, but consider that any commitments he made were to be taken lightly. For that reason she persisted.

"I'm only in Zacatecas for the day. I'm at the airport. I'm sure I could get a cab from here to your office."

"It's quite a distance. It would take maybe half an hour," he temporized, and she knew she had won the first round.

"I'll see you in half an hour, then," she said brightly.

"My pleasure, senora." He conceded his defeat graciously.

The taxi was old and dilapidated, but the driver

was friendly. He offered to show her Zacatecas, but she declined, asking to be taken the most direct route to the Plata Nueva Mine. Skirting the town, she could see the twin-towered cathedral D'oro had spoken of and the cobblestone streets that climbed the hills in the direction of the centuries-old mines.

The mine property was fenced and guarded, but Annie's appearance was enough for entry. As they drove through the gate she thought, *So this is where Jim has been all these long years; yet coming here has been so easy.* From him it would only have taken a phone call. Without that phone call she wouldn't be here now, not even for D'oro if she had not known for sure that Jim would be in South America for another month. Why hadn't he ever called her? Could she be so wrong in her feeling that he cared deeply about her even if he didn't love her as she did him?

Without asking, the driver had turned toward the cluster of whitewashed administration buildings. Annie had deliberately refrained from mentioning the laboratory to either the driver or the guard at the gate. She knew that both the company and the Mexican government regarded the Rodriguez Process as their secret and guarded it jealously. The driver parked in the shade of a two-story building and agreed to wait for her. On foot Annie easily found the laboratory in the cluster of buildings whose doors were open to catch the cooling breeze from the mountains. She paused in the open doorway and knocked lightly on the frame. The man who rushed to meet her was small, well-built, and very handsome in the classic Latin mold.

"Senora Baxter, I am Juan Rodriguez," he greeted her, bowing over the hand she extended to him. "Come into my office, where we can talk." He led her to a small glass-enclosed cubicle barely large enough for a single straight-backed visitor's chair beside the large cluttered desk.

"Tell me about D'oro," he asked, eager as a parent inquiring about an absent child.

Annie duly reported on D'oro's health, the fact that she rode often, and that she spoke of Juan and Maria. Then as tactfully as possible she turned the conversation to D'oro's work and her failure with the process.

"But she has done it many times here in the laboratory," Juan assured her.

"I know, but it will not work for her there. I brought you a sample of the ore and the spectrographic report. Could you check it and see why it does not work? It's very important to her," Annie pleaded. She hoped she would not have to try to explain why it was important to D'oro.

Juan's expressive eyes looked deeply sorrowful. "On my own I would do anything for D'oro, but even though I believe what you say, I cannot do this. It's against company policy."

"Go ahead and do it, Juan. I'll be responsible. The lady is an old friend," said the voice that had existed in her memory and in her heart.

"Jim!" She breathed the name even before she shot out of her chair and turned to face him. She felt as shy as the schoolgirl who had first seen him standing in the doorway of her father's ranch house more than twenty years before and had promptly lost her heart to him. There was much about him that had not changed since that day. His tall broad-shouldered body still moved with the same proud easy grace. He was even more sun bronzed, and the clear gray pools of his penetrating eyes seemed to hold greater depths. As the sun caught the gleaming whiteness of his thick luxurious hair it had the effect of a halo, making her not quite sure whether this was a man or the reincarnation of her dreams.

"Ann, it is you?" he said in that special way in which only he pronounced her name. "You make me believe in time machines the way you have compressed so many long years into so few. Let me look at you." He held out his hands and took both of her hands in his while his eyes absorbed the details of her firm youthful figure, her clear suntanned complexion. Annie was glad that the dire predictions about the effects of sun and wind on a woman's skin had not proved true in her case. Finally his fingers touched the thin white streak in her dark hair.

"You didn't think about missing me as much as I did you."

Startled, she looked up to see that his eyes were laughing as a lock of white hair tumbled over his forehead. They laughed together and threw their arms around each other in a hug that was more an *abrazo* than a romantic embrace.

It was the opening Juan needed to make his exit. "I'll start work on it immediately, senora..." He hesitated as if having difficulty remembering the name he had used minutes before, or trying to place in what connection he might have heard it before.

"Baxter," Annie supplied automatically without diverting any awareness from the look, the feel, the nearness of the man whose strong arms held her close.

"Let's get out of here before I find you're something our mad scientist conjured up in a test tube to enchant me," Jim said. His arm propelled her toward the door.

"It's another planet," she said as she breathed the dry crisp mountain air and looked around her at the sparse vegetation on the red clay slopes of the mountain.

"We call it *Cerro de la Bufa*—Wineskin Mountain. See, there it is, our most important attraction next to the cathedral." He pointed to a formation on top of the mountain that did indeed look like an ancient wineskin.

"My driver pointed out the cathedral on the way from the airport." She was aware that their lips made small talk while their bodies were sending out the important messages of excitement and longing and loving remembrance. His fingers told her fingers, his arm around her conveyed the message to her waist. Her eyes answered his.

"My driver! He's parked in the shade of that two-story building. He'll think that I skipped out on him."

"He'll be sleeping in the shade of his car, confident that you have a siesta-time assignation. They have most civilized customs here." His eyes held speculative amusement that actually made her blush.

His predictions about the driver proved to be correct, but he sprang to life at their approach. The tone of his *"Gracias, señor,"* and roguish wink at Jim was a man-to-man acknowledgment of the charms of the lady he had brought to visit the tall American. He never doubted that it was the object of her visit.

"Juan called you Senora Baxter. They can't both be right," he said, raising a questioning eyebrow.

"I'd feel silly calling myself Senorita Baxter at my age. I don't think they have a translation for ms."

He chuckled appreciatively. "So you never remarried. And what's wrong with your age? I find I no longer have a taste for fruit or wine or women who have not had the time to reach the peak of their perfection."

Annie was amazed at the way the once inarticulate man had acquired a verbal charm to match his physical attraction. He was a prime example of someone maturing well. She wouldn't let herself think about the practice it must have taken to acquire such skill at flattering a woman.

"I think I might have said the same for cars," he said as he led her to the other side of the parking lot and opened the door of a Buick of the original classic design. The car's gleaming black exterior and unmarred fawn-color upholstery gave mute evidence of loving restoration and careful preservation. Her father had driven such a car thirty years earlier.

"I thought you were in South America," she said hesitantly once the well-tuned powerful car was humming its way through the moonlike landscape in the opposite direction from the town.

"I just got back yesterday. An uprising in one of the countries we were to have visited cut our trip short. I knew there was some reason I was hurrying home." His voice began teasing. "So it wasn't me, it was the dashing Latin lover Juan who lured you here?"

Annie started to take the opening to tell him about D'oro, then she recognized that he had been deliberately treating her visit like a lovers' reunion, avoiding all the details of twenty-six years to be talked out later. Perhaps he was right. They had never said the right things when they talked. It was a whole new idea for her. She liked the feel of it. It was indeed a strange enchanted planet, where the proper color for a young man's hair was a gleaming white and forty was the age when a woman reached her peak of desirability and seductiveness. She nestled her head contentedly against his shoulder.

The road dropped into a valley where a grove of tamarisk rose in startling contrast to the surrounding barrenness. In the center of the grove was the final evidence of enchanted madness. The S/S ranch house was sitting there, transported complete.

"Jim, I'm seeing things!" she gasped, not at all sure she wasn't.

He laughed with pleasure. "It was as much of my life as I was able to bring with me."

"Didn't Sally object?" As soon as she asked it she knew why he had avoided speaking what was uppermost in each of their minds. Putting it into words knocked off the scabs that covered old wounds.

"I don't think she really noticed. Sally's interest in the house centered in the mirrors, the closets, and the bath. It made an interesting combination." He said it without rancor as he helped her out of the car. The hand-carved oak door that he opened for her was so like her own that Annie felt that her key would fit its lock.

When the heavy door swung wide, she stepped into a memory. The room looked exactly as the ranch house had twenty-six years earlier. Jim was right about her having arrived in a time machine. As she moved around the room in a near trance she felt as if she really were young again, back in that other room with things the way they should have been. She paused in front of the mantel and picked up an old-fashioned hammered silver candleholder. "Jim, you even have the lady's leg candleholder."

He laughed, and her heart skipped a beat. There had been so little to laugh about when they had last seen each other.

"Like the old silversmith said, it only works if you mind your manners and don't grasp the lady's leg above the ankle." Jim closed his thumb and forefinger around the ankle and ran them suggestively down the small silver leg, hooking his finger as if to snap the tiny cancan garter. His eyes were so pointedly focused on her shapely hips and legs that Annie felt as if she were being caressed.

Annie laughed with delight. What a charmer he had become. He had added polish and wit to all the other things she had loved about him. No wonder he was in demand, as D'oro had said, as the extra man at the dinner parties company owners' wives gave when they were in Zacatecas. She thought with envy of the beautiful sophisticated women who had been his companions on such occasions—yet he had refrained from marrying any of them.

Jim walked over to where she was standing in front of the fireplace and put a cool inviting margarita in her hand. She took a long sip, enjoying the tanginess of lime and salt and the smoothness of orange liqueur blended with tequila. She was surprised when he took the glass from her hand after only one sip and set it on the mantel. He put his arms around her, drawing her close against him. She stood on tiptoe to wrap her arms around his neck. She had forgotten how tall he was. His lips met hers gently, then the tip of his tongue traced the salt from the margarita still clinging to her lips. She could taste the salt on his and she touched her tongue to it and wondered if that was why Mexicans put salt on the rims of margarita glasses. Then she was past the salt to the fire of the tequila igniting in her blood as he continued to kiss her with all the passion and skill and hunger many years apart could build. There was no such thing as time, just the two of them in the magic world he had created—a world that his whole body was saying needed her to be complete.

Jim then raised his head and gently pushed her away from him. "I've wanted to do that for as long as I can remember."

Annie thought of how desperately she had wanted him the last time she had seen him, the day he left Mariposa. Once the decision had been made she had been afraid to even reach out her hand and touch him.

He handed her back her margarita and picked up his own, then he crossed to a big leather couch and sat with his long legs stretched out in front of him. How often she had imagined him sitting on such a couch in such a room, the one where she had been just the previous morning. Could the time from one world to the other have been so short?

"Come sit beside me. I think now we are ready to talk." He patted the cushion beside him. "Where shall we begin?" he asked when she was settled beside him, but not quite touching him. "You mentioned D'oro to Juan. How did you two get together behind my back?" His tone indicated he was not displeased that they had done so.

"You didn't know she was in Mariposa?"

"No. Like I said, I just got in last night. Both Juan and Maria were a little evasive about her whereabouts other than that she was in the United States. I hadn't had time to get the details out of them."

"Is Maria here now?"

"No. While I was gone she had been going

home for siesta. Since I'm alone, I insisted she continue to do so. She'll be back to fix dinner. Now, about D'oro."

"Several years ago I sold the Heartbreaker to a young miner. He found a rich new vein and has been shipping ore to a smelter in Arizona, but he'd like to set up a mill there in Mariposa."

"That makes sense, since there's no longer a smelter operating in California."

"He advertised for a laboratory technician familiar with the Rodriguez Process. D'oro saw it in the mining journal and applied."

He scowled, plainly disturbed. "I should have anticipated something like that when I allowed her to become a metallurgist specializing in silver. Of course I expected her to stay here and work with Juan. There aren't that many places in the U.S. where silver is being mined anymore. I didn't know you were back in production in Mariposa."

"I'm not, but Bret is."

"Bret Harte?" he asked with amusement in his voice in spite of his concern.

"No. Bret Johnson is the man operating the Heartbreaker, but you get the idea."

"But D'oro wasn't able to do the job, and that's why you came down to see Juan?"

Annie nodded, wondering how she would answer the next question she knew was coming.

"Why is the process and the mill so important to you?"

"It isn't. But it is important to D'oro. She's in love with Bret."

"I don't see what that has to do with it. If he's

shipping ore to Arizona, he should be making enough for them to get by on."

"It isn't quite like that. Things haven't progressed that smoothly. She needs time to see if things can be worked out. If her recheck is the failure the original experiment was, and with other pressures, I'm sure she'll just walk away from it. I didn't want that to happen."

"By other pressures you mean the Silver Queen? Did you tell her about the accident?"

"No. I wanted to, but from things she said, I knew you hadn't and I just couldn't seem to find the way."

"You mean how do you tell D'oro that her father could be a murderer? What happened, one of the town gossips tell her?" he said bitterly.

"No. Worse than that. There's a beautiful specimen of ore from the Silver Queen in the museum with your name on it. When the woman in charge didn't know any more about it, D'oro looked it up in back files of the *Gazette*."

"My God! What an awful way to learn about a thing like that." The color had drained from his face and for the moment he looked very old. "I always meant to tell her, but I just never found the way."

"I know," she said, placing her hand comfortingly on his leg. His large hand covered hers appreciatively.

"Wouldn't it be better for her just to forget the whole thing and come home?"

"It isn't something you forget. It's something you accept and learn to live with. The people of

Mariposa haven't changed their mind about you being not guilty. I wish you'd think about coming back.''

"The Naltons are still in Coulterville, aren't they?"

"Yes, but they've shown no inclination to do anything in twenty-six years except file a routine legal claim that was rejected a long time ago. They didn't even raise a protest when Clay was declared legally dead at the time I sold the Heartbreaker.''

"Still, my reappearance could be just the catalyst to set off more violence. God knows there's been enough of that." He gave her a wry grin. "Besides, I doubt if having her father show up is just what D'oro needs for this big romance you're so set on. Tell me about this Bret."

"He's a mining engineer, about thirty. He graduated from Colorado School of Mines. That's where he heard about the Rodriguez Process. He's a lot like you were at that age.''

"When you look at the mess I made of my life and yours, I'm not sure that's any recommendation." He paused. "I meant to come back to you from Vegas, but there was Sally then D'oro . . . and here we are with a lot of water under the bridge. This time I'll accept your judgment. If there's anything I can do, D'oro will have her chance. If Juan can find out why the formula didn't work, he'll let me know. When do you have to go back?"

"I intended to take the late plane tonight. I have a horse entered at Santa Anita tomorrow."

"You have made a success of your work. Don't tell me you're raising Thoroughbreds?"

"No. I'll stick to quarter horses. Every now and then they have a special race for them there." They were back to making small talk while his eyes pleaded with her not to leave him so soon.

"Of course, I don't suppose Megatite could hear me rooting for him in the stands, but I'd have to be there when the race is over if he wins, or they'd send out a search party for me. I think the morning plane would make that."

"Megatite—black, of course? That's where the gold and silver are found. I like that. I wouldn't want to ask you to miss the big race."

Jim leaned over and kissed the tip of her pert nose in an old familiar gesture. "Want to see the rest of the house, check how good my memory was?" He got up and took her hand.

"This is D'oro's room," he said as they stood in the doorway of a room so like the one D'oro was then occupying that Annie started to giggle.

"No wonder she looked startled when I showed her my guest room." They laughed together until tears rolled down their cheeks. The situation wasn't really that funny, but the tensions that it relieved had been that great.

"I'll let Maria show you the kitchen when she gets back. It's her pride and joy. But don't mention D'oro yet. Tonight I want you all to myself. Tell her tomorrow when I go over to the laboratory to check with Juan. Then the two of you can cluck over your shared chick."

Recalling Juan's eagerness at mention of D'oro's name, Annie agreed.

Putting his arm around her waist, he led her in

the direction where the master bedroom ought to have been, and was. She walked slowly around the room, reveling in his male presence in myriad small details: his brushes on the dresser; the fresh woodsy smell of his after-shave lotion, which hung in the air; the characteristic neatness in the way things were placed.

"It's right in every detail," she said as her fingers traced the hand-carved design on the headboard of the king-size bed.

"It looks the same, but I'm not sure. I never had the opportunity to try the other one." He said it lightly in a tone imitating a customer in a furniture store. The images his words called up were not funny or light. They brought back some very ugly ghosts. Damn words! she thought.

But Jim had the words to wipe out the ill-chosen ones. He sat down on the edge of the bed. "You'll have to be the expert to judge if it's right." He patted the place on the bed beside him.

Gratefully she picked up the game. She sat on the bed, ran her hands over its surface, bounced lightly on the springs, and said, "Feels right."

"You can't judge by such a superficial test," he said, gently pushing her backward until she was lying on the bed. His lips touched the feather of white hair at her temple, brushed her eyelids above her long sweeping eyelashes, then traced the contour of her cheek to her waiting mouth. Like a little girl, she kicked off her shoes. Jim's arms scooped her up and swung her around so that her head rested on the pillow. Somewhere in the process she lost her slacks. She didn't quite know what happened to her shirt, but her eager hands helped him remove his, then his big gentle hands were exploring her body as his lips had explored her face, as if checking the reality against his memory. Like a magnet his gleaming halo of hair drew her fingers to it, caressing, reveling in its silky crispness.

"Not a single lovely particle of you has changed from the way I've remembered you all these years. Ann, I love you." He said it again and again as if to make up for the times he had not said it.

How many years had it been since anyone had called her Ann? No one had ever said it quite the way he did, his lips so close to hers, she could feel his warm breath. She only had to pucker her lips to touch his and invite his mouth to join hers. As his hands moved expertly over her body it was as if she were a doll coming back to life in a magic fairy tale. They made love hungrily like people who hadn't eaten in a very long time, then with the incredible lassitude of being completely satisfied, Annie slept in his arms.

When she awakened, his clear gray eyes were studying her face as if to burn a photographic memory into his mind. As soon as he was aware she was awake the corners of his eyes crinkled in amusement. "Good cure for jet lag. I'll have to remember that on my next long trip."

She bristled in anger, then realized he was teasing her. He kissed her lightly on the tip of her nose. "I'll get your suitcase from the car. I wasn't sure which room to put it in when we arrived," he said, grinning at her.

"You're awful. A positive seducer, and in broad daylight," she teased, feeling young and giddy and boundlessly alive.

"What did you think they have siestas for?"

When the door clicked behind him, she slid out of the big bed and padded across the room to where a door stood slightly ajar into the semidarkness of the bathroom. As soon as she stepped through the door the room was flooded with soft pink light, and she found her nude body reflected back from softly tinted mirrors on every wall. She began to giggle helplessly. It was the perfect room for the completely ego-centered female. She crossed the room with a dozen of her own images following her from various angles. At the far side she found a sunken pink ceramic tile tub almost as large as the big bed she had just left. If you dropped the soap, you might have to swim for it, she thought as she started water cascading from golden fixtures into the tub. She wondered how it all had been managed in such a remote small town in Mexico, then she recalled what an excellent engineer Jim was. She could see what he meant about Sally's part of the house. Still, she felt no jealousy. It seemed to her that in his own way Jim had been laughing at the woman he married when he built it.

After the most luxurious bath she could remember, Ann wrapped herself in a large pink velour bath sheet. In the confusing hall of mirrors she found a door opposite the one she had entered, which led to another room from which she had heard sounds. It was a frilly pink dressing room. Her suitcase stood on a stool beside the open closet door. She was glad she had expected to be back at Santa Anita by the end of the race and that she had faith in Megatite. She had packed her winner's celebration dress.

Annie slipped into frilly lingerie—her secret self-assertion that she was a woman in a largely male-dominated business. She applied with care makeup she seldom used and probably wouldn't have brought along except for the dress: a soft muted brown eyeshadow that made her sparkling eyes appear even larger, a hint of rose blusher, a soft and creamy rose lipstick. Then she dropped over her head the shimmering old-gold lamé evening dress that fit her curves like a second skin.

Jim was standing beside the big leather couch, pouring margaritas into salt-rimmed glasses, when she entered the living room. His action froze when he saw her, and Annie was afraid he would allow the clear liquid to run over the top of one glass. He frowned. "I'm afraid there is no place in Zacatecas I can take you to merit such glamour."

"I thought you said we would be dining here. The dress isn't for a place, it's for an occasion. I wear it to celebrate when I've had a winner. Today I've had a winner."

His laugh started from somewhere deep in his throat and filled the room with warmth. "I had forgotten what a delight you are, besides being so beautiful after all this time. I don't know whether I wish I could show you off to the whole world or treasure you to myself like a Midas counting his gold in secret.'' Some of the over-filled liquid spilled on his hand. ''See what you've made me do!'' He sipped the drink down to a safe level and set it back on the padded leather bar while he poured hers. ''Now, don't go away. I'll be right back,'' he assured her as he headed in the direction of the master bedroom. He paused at the door as if he had just remembered something. Looking back, he asked, ''You can sit down in that dress, can't you?''

Annie hated to think how much her laugh sounded like a giggle.

Jim returned in minutes, wearing a white dinner jacket that did breathtaking things for his broad shoulders and a maroon cummerbund that made his lean, hard waist seem almost sinful. He still wore the pale gray slacks and fine white linen shirt that he had originally selected for dinner.

''Can't let our visitors think we're country cousins,'' he said, picking up his drink and toasting her with his eyes.

A middle-aged Mexican woman arrived from the kitchen. She had a smiling serene face and large intelligent dark eyes. She looked from one to the other in dismay.

''You did not tell me dinner was formal, *señor*. Will there be others? I thought you said we had *una visita*?''

''Maria, this is Senorita Baxter. Tonight we're celebrating a winner, just the two of us. Don't worry, all of your dinners are fit for a celebration.''

Maria beamed at his praise. She didn't expect to understand those crazy North Americans. Of the whole confusing business, the only part she understood was that the senor would want to dine alone with the beautiful senorita. "Welcome, *señorita,*" she said with genuine warmth.

"I'm happy to meet you, Maria. I've heard a lot about you," Annie replied, but catching the warning signal from Jim's eyes did not say from whom she had heard about her.

"Dinner is served," Maria said with a knowing smile.

The dining room showed the Mexican's love of things romantic. A long runner and a decorative centerpiece of silk flowers and candles on the table made it appear that the remaining end was a separate table set for two. The dark polished wood and gleaming Taxco silver on the sideboard were in fact a most appropriate setting for the two elegantly dressed diners. Over dinner Jim flirted with Annie as outrageously as any Latin caballero, holding her hand between courses of Maria's sumptuous meal.

Afterward they sipped orange liqueur in the living room and bridged the years of separation with reminiscence and gossip about mutual acquaintances. They talked until late into the night, then they made love again, this time savoring each precious moment of the other's pleasure.

Annie awakened with a lovely languorous glow suffusing her whole body. She stretched, luxurious as a tawny cat. She reached out her hand to the pillow beside her own, but found only the indentation where a precious head had been. For a moment it seemed to her that her recurring dream had only been more real last night. She took a deep breath and smelled the lingering scent of woody after-shave. She was in his room, not hers! He had slipped out without waking her. She hadn't slept like that in years.

Annie freshened up and dressed quickly in a pencil-slim skirt and a sheer white cotton blouse. She had brought the outfit in case lunch with Juan had been the only possible contact. She walked out through the French doors onto the patio and leaned against a deep-set window, enjoying the invigorating effect of the fresh dry mountain air. The musical sound of Spanish drifted up to her from where two gardeners were working below the crest of the hill.

"El Blanco has found his woman," the unseen voice was saying.

So among themselves the Mexicans called Jim El Blanco. She could well imagine the awe with which the workers regarded the powerful, virile man with the snow-white hair, and she felt sure it had been that way since his arrival in Mexico or not too long thereafter. But why had those workmen concluded that she was his woman? She knew other women would have spent the night with him since Sally's departure. Puzzled, she turned back toward her room. The slanting rays of the morning sun had made a mirror of the window behind her, sending back her reflection. Her hand flew to the white streak in her own hair. In the mysticism of Mexico that must surely have been a sign of destiny. El Blanco had found his woman.

With a smile of contentment Annie crossed the patio to the kitchen entrance. Maria offered to bring her breakfast out on the patio, but Annie said she would eat in the kitchen. Then she mentioned the magic word *D'oro,* and all distinction of nationality and position disappeared as the two honorary aunts compared notes about their favorite niece.

When Jim returned, Juan was with him.

"I'm sorry, *señorita.* It didn't work. I don't know why. I checked everything very carefully." One look at Juan's tired face, and she knew he had worked most of the night on the sample she had brought. His eyes held that peculiar kind of scientific curiosity that told her he would keep at it until he did know why. She wasn't sure the answer would arrive soon enough to save anything for D'oro but her pride.

"Thank you, Juan. It was good of you to do this. I think it will reassure D'oro to learn that the failure was not due to a mistake on her part."

"Give her our love. Tell her we miss her," said Juan.

"*Sí,* " added Maria with an emphatic nod to endorse what Juan had said. "*Via con Dios.* " She added her good wishes for Annie.

Seeing the love and concern in the expressive dark eyes of the brother and sister, Annie knew that D'oro was truly their golden one. She shook hands with Juan and received an affectionate *abrazo* from Maria. When the shiny black Buick drove through the gate of Plata Nueva Mine, the time had come to tell Jim of her decision.

"If you don't think it's wise to come to Mariposa, I'll sell the ranch or lease it and come here." She said it as if it were a carefully rehearsed speech.

Jim looked at her with a slow smile and said gently, "I can't let you do that. What about that winner at Santa Anita? The ranch and horses are your life's work."

"Some life without you."

"You'd get bored in Zacatecas. We haven't the pasture or facilities for raising horses. There isn't much for an active woman to do here. You'd miss your friends and all the things you've always known."

"Like Sally?"

"You know I didn't mean that," he said, dropping his hand from the steering wheel to cover hers.

"I must have some talent that would be useful in Zacatecas."

"I can think of several." His smile was intimate and suggestive, bringing heightened color to her cheeks, then his face became thoughtful. "You are the most self-sufficient woman I have ever known. I have been meeting your generous offer with flimsy excuses. You have a right to be told the truth."

He was silent several minutes, then he began in a low controlled voice, "Clay was already down in the shaft that Monday morning when I returned from Los Angeles. Looking down, I could see the light on his hat, but I couldn't see his face. He could see me. There was almost a challenge in the way he waved his miners' light for me to start the hoist. Watching him, I thought of what he had done to you and I wished the bastard dead and in hell. In minutes he was, and by my hand.''

Annie sat so still, she scarcely breathed, dreading what she feared he would say next.

Jim seemed to be searching for the right words to make her understand. "I didn't cut the cable. If I was to decide a man had to die, that wouldn't be my way. You knew that—the jury understood it. But I was operating the hoist. I was an experienced miner, yet I didn't see the nearly unraveled cable. Perhaps subconsciously I didn't want to see it. The jury found me not guilty. I have never been able to do so.''

How could she have failed to comprehend how a responsible, caring man like Jim would feel about Clay's death? God help her, there had been a time when part of her had hoped that Jim killed Clay for her. How could she have been so immature and stupid? But that had been a long time ago. Softly she asked, "Don't you think you've paid enough for any part you may have had in the accident?''

"Clay is dead, and I'm alive. No man has a right on his own to pass judgment and decide who deserves to die. I cannot compound my guilt by marrying his widow, though you are the only woman I have ever loved." He gave her hand a final squeeze and returned his hand to the steering wheel, which he gripped so hard, his knuckles showed white.

Annie clenched her hands in her lap and fought

back the tears. They did not speak again until they were in the airport terminal, safely insulated by other people.

"Give my love to D'oro. Sorry we couldn't solve her problem, either," he said when the boarding gate was opened. He brushed her cheek lightly with his lips. When she would have turned and thrown herself into his arms, she found herself being carried through the gate by the press of other passengers behind her. At the top of the boarding stairs she turned back to catch a glimpse of proud broad shoulders and an erect white head above the crowd of shorter Mexicans. She knew she had lost him to the very qualities that she loved in him: his honor, his pride, and his strength.

Chapter Nine

On Thursday morning D'oro had watched Annie and Rattlesnake load the nervous young horse in the van for the big race at Santa Anita before she drove to the mine. Thor met her with the enthusiasm of a long-lost friend.

"He isn't here, is he?" she asked as if they both understood the other's problem. D'oro raced the handsome black dog back to the mine, where the absence of Bret's pickup confirmed her assumption that he was gone. Thor had fresh food and water, but that didn't necessarily mean that Bret had been home the previous night. Someone else might look after Thor in Bret's absence. If he had gone to see Candy, he might have been reluctant to ask D'oro to do it.

The day's work might as well have been done by a robot. Each element responded to her tests exactly as it had the first time. Through the long morning D'oro tested, measured, checked, and observed. As the hands of her watch dragged slowly toward noon she picked up a multicolored piece of peacock copper and dropped it into a beaker of nitric acid. She watched as the glowing blue, purple, green, and bronze leached out into the liquid, forming a shimmering rainbow, then dulled to a uniform rust. She marked her check sheet as before and decided to break for lunch. She took her brown-bag lunch to the shade of a tree and shared it with Thor. Both of their appetites were affected by Bret's absence. She played catch with the lonesome dog, then returned dispiritedly to her work.

The afternoon dragged interminably as she checked off the remaining minerals on the spectrograph. By the time she was ready for the final step she could anticipate the results. She had found no difference in any of the elements. With a sense of futility she dropped the zinc pellets into the aqua regia. They slowly slithered through the solution in the test tube, but there was no following shower of silver particles. She had failed to produce the formula Bret needed for his mill! She felt a desperate urge to fling the offending test tube against the wall. Instead, like a well-trained automaton, she dumped the results of her work into the waste disposal and began cleaning up the laboratory. She was glad Bret had not been there to witness her final failure, but she longed for his comforting presence, for him to put his arms around her and assure her that her failure didn't matter in his feeling for her. Could that be the reason he asked her to go to Yosemite with him, away from the whole mining scene? He would be back to keep their date, wouldn't he?

After a night of fitful sleep, D'oro was up early. Eager as a schoolgirl, she taunted herself as she dressed carefully in a pearl-gray pantsuit and coordinated pink-and-gray blouse that emphasized the unusual color of her clear gray eyes. She used the sash from the blouse as a headband to tie back her long blond hair. She was just finishing the slice of toast and cup of coffee she had forced herself to eat when she was startled by a knock at the door. She hadn't heard the familiar sound of Bret's pickup in the driveway.

When she answered the door, she found herself mirrored in the approving eyes of a relaxed and smiling Bret. He wore perfectly tailored designer jeans, topped by a silver-gray suede cloth shirt open at the throat. He looked like a wealthy playboy-rancher, not a working miner.

"That's my lady, ready without being called." He reminded her of their private joke when they had ridden to Hidden Valley. He kissed her lightly with a suggestion that the day was just beginning.

"Many are called, but few are chosen." She picked up the thread of the joke and smiled up at him as he helped her into her jacket. When they stepped off the enclosed porch, D'oro was startled to see that it was Annie's silver Porsche, not Bret's pickup, that was parked by the front gate. She reacted by turning a questioning look at Bret and immediately regretted that her expressive eyes revealed what she was thinking.

"I thought the Porsche would be more comfortable than the truck today. Annie says I should use it whenever she takes her horse van."

There was no denying the comfort of the
leather bucket seats, but D'oro felt a strange
sense of discomfort about the arrangement. Was
it another symbol that Bret was leaving behind
any connection with the mine for a purely social
pursuit? He started the powerful motor, backed
the car in a graceful arc, and moved expertly
through the gears as the sleek automobile acceler-
ated smoothly over the country road. There was
no doubt he drove Annie's car with practiced
ease. Suddenly it occurred to D'oro how perfectly
the sophisticated silver automobile fitted with the
other examples of his preference for things that
were silver. He seemed to read her thoughts.

"I used to own the Silver Streak back in my
misspent youth, before I became a mining man,"
he said with mock regret.

"Your youth was misspent at Colorado School
of Mines, studying to become a mining engineer?" she challenged.

He laughed. "Let's say I was referring to the
weekends when the Silver Streak and I really
burned up the road to Denver. Would you settle
for worked hard, played hard?"

"I'll buy that." In the varied moods in which
she had seen him, he had devoted boundless en-
ergy to whatever he was doing. "Juan has told me
about the work to become a mining engineer. Tell
me about the play."

He gave her a crooked grin. "As he probably
told you, School of Mines is at Golden, in the
mountains, so there was skiing in the winter and
trail riding in the summer."

She had seen him on horseback, and what a magnificent figure he must cut on skis. Of course, neither of those activities would involve frequent trips to Denver in the Silver Streak, as he spoke of the Porsche. Each of them was willing to let the subject drop at that. For that one day she was determined to think of nothing except the pleasure of the moment. Bret's hand slipped from the steering wheel to cover hers, and her only awareness was of him and the excitement his touch aroused in her whole being.

The familiar sign marking the turnoff to the Heartbreaker Mine intruded on her contented glow. Bret made no comment, but it seemed strange to D'oro to be so disinterestedly passing the familiar route in the elegant sporty Porsche Bret had given or traded to Annie. Had it been part of the deal for the mine, or was it a more personal transaction? D'oro had recognized from the start the deep bond of affection between Bret and Annie. Had she been naive in her evaluation of their relationship? There was little doubt that Annie had been in love with her father. Bret was like him in many ways. Although Annie was considerably older than Bret, there was no denying she was a very attractive, charming, sophisticated woman. Was the open flaunting of his affair with Candy merely a cover for a deeper relationship with Annie? D'oro miserably considered that possible complication of her problem. She would readily seize any opportunity to win Bret away from Candy, but could she if the other woman was Annie?

Through lowered lashes she studied him. His thick curling hair made her fingers itch to tangle themselves in it. His rugged handsome face was relaxed and smiling. The controlled power of his broad shoulders and arms and the skill of his hands gave him easy mastery of the Porsche. He handled it with the same combination of deftness and sensitivity that would give him mastery over a woman. How could she leave such a man when she wanted him so much? She had no choice. Everything about the day made it clear that it was to be a final *hasta mañana.*

D'oro resolved to match Bret's carefree manner. She set her small chin defiantly, painted on her most dazzling smile, and turned flirtatiously toward him.

"Did you see that squirrel?" he asked, removing his hand from hers to point out the blur of red-brown fur that scurried across the road in front of them.

She turned to look back over her shoulder at the squirrel perched impudently on the side of the road, chattering his displeasure at their intrusion. He emphasized his complaints with swishing movements of his beautiful tail.

"I guess he's telling you off." They laughed together in a companionship that they had rarely managed to achieve. His arm had been around her shoulders when she turned from looking back at the squirrel, and she resented the comfortable bucket seats, which enforced the separation between them. Forcing herself to concentrate on the scenery, she had to admit it was magnificent. Red clay hills were patterned with cinnamon-colored grass and the hulking green bulk of live oak trees. The contorted forms of red-barked manzanita invited the imagination to see figures of fantasy.

"Did you bring your fishing pole?" he asked as he returned the friendly wave of a fisherman standing knee-deep in the clear tumbling water of the Merced River, whose scenic valley they were then following.

"No, but I'll bait your hook," she countered.

"I thought it was supposed to work the other way. What ever happened to women who were afraid to put a worm on a hook?"

"I've blown my lines again." His amused eyes sought hers, and they laughed together more from the promise of the day stretching before them than from the light pleasantries they exchanged.

Sooner than she would have liked D'oro saw a dramatic granite formation like the prow of a giant ship that she recognized from pictures as El Portal, guardian of the gateway to Yosemite. Bret drove through the Arch Rock entrance and stopped to give her a full view of the dramatically balanced rock formation.

"Looks like the slightest jolt would topple the rock across the top," she said.

"It does look precariously balanced, yet it was not disturbed by nearby severe earthquakes."

"I've never experienced an earthquake. They must be frightening." She stared at the massive boulders and her vivid imagination pictured them teetering in a quake. Suddenly the world around her began to vibrate. She flung her arms around Bret's neck, and he locked his arms protectively around her. As she nestled against the haven of his broad chest she detected a rumbling beneath her ear that was strangely like suppressed laughter. When she looked up into his dancing blue eyes, there could be no question about it. Then she realized he was causing the vibration somehow by manipulating the electric adjustment control on her seat.

"Very funny," she snapped, but his laughter was too infectious to resist, and she joined him.

"Now you are an initiated Californian," he said as he put the car in gear and started up the narrow canyon. In spite of Bret's expert driving D'oro found herself holding the armrest and catching her breath as she looked over the sharp dropoff from the highway to the Merced River cascading through a rocky gorge dozens of feet below. The gorge widened, and Bret parked among ancient pines that dwarfed mere mortals to insignificance. Hand in hand they hiked the short distance to Bridalveil Falls.

"Pure silver lace." Bret sighed with exaggerated rapture.

"It is beautiful, so delicate and filmy," she agreed.

"There's an updraft that whips the water into that lacy spray. There's more water in the spring, but I like the effect we have now after the first rains of fall, particularly when the sun is shimmering off the drops of water."

"Polishes the silver," she teased.

"Now that you're an earthquake veteran you might be interested to know that the place near the top that looks newly chiseled did break off during the quake."

As they drove on toward Yosemite Lodge they seemed to be almost alone in the magnificent wilderness.

"During the summer the valley is crawling with people. The season is past now, and you can get the feel of what it was like in the early days. I keep intending to borrow the horse van and bring Silver up here during the off-season—really get the feeling of discovery."

D'oro smiled to herself as he confirmed her picture of him as pioneer and empire builder in that land, which still challenged the strength and ingenuity of a man. For a brief moment she imagined the happiness of riding Bonanza beside him on such an adventure, then the bubble burst and she recalled that it was her last day in Mariposa.

While she was still trying to shut out thoughts of the future and regain the spirit of the day, he provided the answer by parking in the exact spot where the delicate dramatic rock formation known as Cathedral Spires was a breathtaking delight.

"This really is a fairyland."

"Positively enchanting," he agreed, though his eyes seemed to be more on her eager face than on the spectacle in front of them.

The next stop was a sunny meadow where he helped her from the car and produced a picnic basket from its trunk.

"It can't be lunchtime already," she protested.

"Never argue with a mining man's instincts about when to eat a meal."

Laughing, she glanced at her watch and found that he was right. Where had the morning gone?

He removed the red-and-white-checked tablecloth to reveal a loaf of crusty sourdough bread, ham sliced paper thin, rich golden cheese, bright red apples, and a bottle of sparkling white wine. "'A jug of wine . . . a loaf of bread . . . and thou beside me in the wilderness . . .'" he quoted.

"The Rubaiyat of Omar Khayyàm," she supplied.

"That must be quite a library your father has. Were you born in Mexico?"

"Missed by a few months. I was born in California." For a fleeting moment she was tempted to tell him of the tragedy that had sent her family to Mexico, but she didn't feel the story was hers to tell. She had wondered if he was the one who had checked the *Mariposa Gazette* for that period just before she did. If so, he apparently had not noticed the announcement of her birth. His question seemed to be only idle curiosity.

The tasty lunch occupied their attention. The only sounds were the sighing of the breeze in the pines and the distant ripple of running water. Bret stretched out on his back in the tall grass while D'oro cleared away the few remains of their picnic.

"I could just lie here contented all afternoon if there wasn't so much I still want to show you," he said indolently. That was a new side to Bret, who always seemed so energetic. He held out his hand to her. She took it to help him up, but with a quick twist Bret pulled her down into the cradle of his arms. The tang of the wine still lingered on his lips when they met hers. He kissed her as if her mouth held the greater sweetness. Her blood flamed like it had been a fiery brandy she had drunk, not a cool white wine. Her arms went around his neck and her fingers tangled in his curly dark hair as they had so often itched to do. When his lips left hers to trace the graceful contour of her throat, she softly blew a blade of grass from his cheek and heard the sharp intake of his breath. His mouth moved to the open V of her shirt. His tongue traced the outline of the opening, making little darting forays beneath the edge to the burgeoning top of her breasts. His hand moved to the button of her shirt and stopped, then slid down to span her slender waist and trace the rounded contour of her hips. He seemed determined not to rush her after the fiasco of Hidden Valley.

Bret propped himself up on one elbow and looked down at her with eyes half-hidden from her by lowered eyelids and thick dark lashes. "Your eyes are pure silver. I've looked for it everywhere but in a woman's eyes. You know silver is my weakness." He said it with a surprising ring of truth.

"Then maybe I should have my hair bleached silver."

"Like Candy's?" he asked alertly. "That's not pure silver, only silver plate. The best silver always has some gold with it. You should know that. But silver or gold, I like things natural."

"Is that why you passed up a good natural Mexican dinner for whatever you do with silver plate the other night?" she challenged, half afraid it would end their day as it was just beginning.

Instead of being angry he only laughed. "That sounds like jealousy talking. Maybe there's some Mexican fire under that cool exterior, after all. It wasn't really a choice. I don't think you would have been amused by the show Candy would have put on if I had stood her up to have dinner with you. But don't tell Thor. He'd never forgive me for passing up an invitation for a good Mexican dinner." He cupped her face and lightly kissed each eyelid. She held her breath, waiting for his mouth to return to hers. Instead his arm beneath her shoulders gently raised her to a sitting position, then he helped her to her feet. Whatever he had in mind for the day, she guessed the time was not yet right.

Bret put the picnic basket back in the car and took her hand, leading her along a path marked "Mirror Lake." The trees became thicker, and small animals darted across their path while bright birds flashed between the branches. A warning press of his fingers stopped her as he pointed to a small stream where a soft-eyed doe and her fawn drank. It was an Eden from which D'oro wished she never need return.

At the top of a gently sloping hill the green shade of the pines was pierced by shafts of golden sunlight, then they were once more in the open beneath the incredibly blue sierra sky. In front of them was a glass-smooth lake. Its clear water reflected the blue of the sky above it, and in the center a rugged snow-capped mountain peak. It was well named Mirror Lake.

"Oh, Bret, it's beautiful."

He slipped his arm around her and drew her forward to the edge of the water. His image smiled back at her like an ancient god beneath the waters of a mystic sea. The blue of his eyes seemed to have concentrated the essence of sky and water.

"See, I've caught me a mermaid." He laughed with a rich deep sound that reverberated through her.

D'oro's reflection with his arm around her did look a little like a mermaid. Her long blond hair was mirrored above a patch of moss, and a protruding boulder cut the reflection just above the knees. She hoped he didn't know how completely he had captured her. She looked at the perfect unspoiled beauty surrounding them and wondered if that was where he planned to make love to her. Her pulse began to quicken at the thought. She did not delude herself that he loved her, but back in the meadow it had been quite clear that he wanted her. She loved him so desperately, she knew she must at least have that day to remember in her exile.

Bret turned her into the circle of his arms and drew her to him. His lips met hers in a kiss that was cool and gentle, then seemed to find the fire that was pulsing through her. When she put her arms around his neck, he was so tall, she found herself standing on tiptoe, the softness of her body conforming to the lean hard lines of his. His hands moved down her slender body in a slow caress. They teased the tips of her firm breasts, glided over the tightened muscles of her slender waist, and locked behind her rounded hips. Her response to him was as natural and primitive as the unspoiled wilderness in which they stood. Slowly he raised his mouth from hers and looked deep into her eyes as if to confirm the response her body was offering his.

"Your eyes are mirrors like the lake. I can almost see myself in them the way I've wanted to since the first time I discovered your eyes are silver. Today they're shining like coins newly minted." Bret's finger touched the bridge of her nose and traced the arch of her eyebrow with feather lightness, then completed the oval beneath her lower lid. With a quick motion he bunched his fingers together as if he were trying to capture an elusive prize and then tucked it in the pocket of his shirt above his heart.

Happiness bubbled up in D'oro's laugh, and his mouth caught hers in shared delight. His kiss explored her soft mouth, seeking more treasure to make his own. She knew it was more than the gleam in her eye he had tucked into his pocket. It was her heart as well. She could feel it beating there close against the strong drumbeat of his, causing the blood to surge through her veins each time he moved his deft hands over her enraptured body.

She had never dreamed it was possible to love a

man, to want a man as desperately as she loved and wanted Bret. Though he did not offer her commitment, there could be no doubt he wanted her as desperately as she wanted him. The setting had been well chosen, and she knew his lovemaking would be as flawless.

He tightened his arms beneath her hips and lifted her as if she were a mermaid he was taking from the lake. With her head above his, she bent to trace the chiseled bone structure of his face with little feathered kisses from her passion-softened lips. Her mouth reached his and she was kissing him, or was he kissing her?

Though she felt as if she had stopped breathing, he was first to turn his mouth away. He cocked his head on one side in a listening pose, then she heard it too, stealthy, heavy steps approaching through the trees. Noiselessly he lowered her to the ground and turned to face the sound, one arm still protectively around her shoulders.

With total nonchalance a large brown bear emerged from the trees and lumbered down to the water's edge for a drink.

"Is he dangerous?" D'oro whispered.

"Not unless you smell of bacon." Bret laughed, a note of huskiness edging his voice. "The way he ignores our presence, he's one of the garbage-can bears, banished up here when he became a nuisance in the valley."

"He is a handsome brute," she said, admiring the bear's massive head and thickening autumn coat.

"Now I'm jealous," he teased. "But I wouldn't

want to dispute his claim in case he feels we're trespassing." With his arm lightly around her waist they returned to the meadow where they had left the car.

They drove around the loop road where the glowing reds of oak trees mingled with the gold of aspen along the streams. A few tourists still strolled through Yosemite Village and along the path to Yosemite Falls, which was their destination.

"What a magnificent waterfall!" D'oro craned her neck to look up at the crescent of water breaking over the white granite cliff and cascading in breathtaking stages to the river they were crossing.

"*Deafening* is the word when the full force of the spring runoff from the snowpack begins tumbling down that cliff."

They climbed to the first pool where the falls hesitated in its downward rush. There mist rising from the falls left sparkling jewels of water on the white granite. They followed a different path through brilliant fall foliage and cool evergreens until they were again on the valley floor. One path led to another, opening to D'oro's delighted eyes dramatic vistas of towering peaks and a natural wonderland. It seemed the perfect setting for the rugged independent man sharing it with her.

"I'm getting hungry. How about you?" Bret asked as they emerged from a thick pine grove.

D'oro was surprised to find that the sun had dropped behind the ridge of a granite mountain with the suddenness of an autumn day in the high country.

"I hadn't thought about eating until you mentioned it. Where has the day gone so quickly?" she asked regretfully.

"You've enjoyed it, then?"

"It's been perfect," she answered, meaning every word. She realized that had been his intention, to give her a beautiful memory of the last hours she would spend with him. She wanted to cry out in protest that it couldn't end like that, but she knew that it would. In the deepening gloom of twilight and her own depressed thoughts there was still some ray of light. The day was not yet over. She resolved to make the most of every precious minute that remained.

Catching that last mood, Bret tucked her arm through his as they walked along the nearly deserted road back to where he had parked the car. A curving path through spectacularly tall pines ended abruptly in front of the beautiful stone Awahnee Hotel, integrated into its setting by time.

"Pretend we arrived in a Stanley steamer." Bret opened the door of the cathedral-ceilinged hotel, which still retained the elegance of the 1920s. Polished hardwood floors framed colorful Indian rugs. Massive wrought-iron chandeliers high overhead gave the whole a soft glow, mellowing the heavy golden oak tables and rich natural leather upholstery.

The maître d' appraised Bret and his companion with a practiced eye and led them to a choice table for two, framed by a twenty-foot ceiling-to-floor window with a dramatic view of granite domes beyond. Bret selected their dinner of chilled melon, trout fresh from the stream with an almondine sauce, accompanied by snow peas and fresh mushrooms. A light white wine accompanied dinner. The service and appointments reminded D'oro of Spanish colonial establishments in Mexico. The waiters wore formal attire, the linen was starched and snowy white, and the silver was so heavy, it might well have been from Taxco. When their dessert arrived, D'oro was reminded of home. It was a creamy flan even Maria would have been proud of.

After dinner they wandered through the souvenir shops that adjoined the lobby. Bret seemed to be searching for something as he ran his eyes expertly over the displays. Finally in the last shop he found it—a small delicate silver filigree butterfly.

"It's called *La Mariposa*," the clerk said as she removed the exquisite piece from the counter for their inspection.

Bret and D'oro exchanged smiles as the clerk bent to close the case. When she turned back to them, Bret was already placing the money on the counter.

"Shall I wrap it?" The clerk smiled with pleased surprise at making the sale so easily. She appraised Bret with new interest.

"No need." He held out his hand for the pendant, slipped the slender chain around D'oro's neck, and fastened it with easy movements of his competent hands, leaving a tingling glow of pleasure where they touched her nape. The clerk held up a mirror for D'oro's inspection.

"It matches your eyes," Bret said with approval.

D'oro knew the glow in her eyes did not come from the lovely silver butterfly resting on the golden suntan of her throat. With fingertips touching lightly they walked out into the incredible starlit night. A slender crescent of silvery moon enhanced the brilliance of the stars in the thin clear air.

As Bret held the car door open for her and helped her in, his lips brushed D'oro's temple with a light tantalizing touch. There was a valley-of-the-moon quality about Yosemite at night, with the glacier-hewn white granite cliffs taking on grotesque shapes against the sky. D'oro felt a communication of mood between them that needed no words as they drove the nearly deserted road. She half closed her eyes, pretending to doze as she studied Bret driving the powerful sports car with such easy command. The soft starlight shadowed his well-defined features, giving them interesting new dimensions. His long slender hands rested with easy competence on the steering wheel. As she watched their skillful movements she could feel again the excitement of those hands caressing her body.

Bret was everything D'oro had always wanted in a man. He had the brilliant mind of an engineer, the hard muscular body of a miner, and the ambition of an empire builder. She realized she had been drawn to him like a magnet from their first encounter.

The familiar sign for Heartbreaker Mine forced

her to face the reality that there were only precious minutes left of their last day together. There was so much she wanted to say to him, but the words eluded her.

His hand found hers and he lifted it to his lips and planted a kiss in the palm of her hand. The warmth of his lips rekindled the flame that sent a glow throughout her entire body. She closed her hand tightly as if to prevent something precious from escaping.

Bret parked near the front walk, opened her door, and half helped, half lifted her into his arms. The moment for which the entire day had been destined had arrived. His lips met hers in a kiss that was tender, persuasive, masterful, and complete. He pressed her slender body against him as if he too were trying to hold on to something precious he feared might slip away from him.

All her longing loneliness exploded in D'oro's desire for the man whose very breathing had become a part of her own. His hands moved over her as if memorizing every curve of her rounded hips, her full breasts. With burning certainty she knew she had to have Bret. She would not let the moment slip through her fingers as Annie and her father had so many years ago.

Sensing her acceptance, Bret slowly separated his mouth from hers. Kissing her lightly on the tip of her nose, he set her on her feet. She was scarcely aware of touching the ground as he guided her willing footsteps to the front door.

D'oro opened her shoulder bag to search for

the key. As she did so Bret withdrew his key ring from his pocket and unlocked the door. A perverse beam of moonlight glinted from the key and from the distinctive key to the Porsche dangling beside it. The suspicion that had first planted itself in her mind when she learned Annie's car had once been Bret's wriggled out of the corner of her brain where she had kept it hidden away all day. The fact that he also had the key to Annie's door made it all too clear that they had been lovers, perhaps still were. D'oro felt not so much betrayed as betrayer. She simply could not do that to Annie, who had given her trust and friendship and an indefinable something more. She could not accept the love of a man whom Annie held dear in Annie's own house.

Bret, who seemed attuned to her every thought, allowed his arm around her to relax. He opened the door and slowly withdrew his key. Perhaps he too was reluctant to make love to another woman under Annie's roof. In a voice husky with emotion he asked softly, "Will you be coming back to the lab tomorrow?"

"My work is finished there." She managed to get the words out with enough steadiness for him to hear.

"I know," he answered with understanding. It was the first time either of them had mentioned the final failure in the laboratory.

D'oro felt as if fate were offering her one more chance. "I planned to come in tomorrow and type up the results of my findings in case you have some future use for the information." It was something she should do; she just hadn't thought about doing it until that moment.

"Why not wait until afternoon and have dinner with me when you finish? I haven't shown you what an accomplished chef I am." He said it casually, but his eyes as they searched hers were dark pools of emotion.

"I'd like that," she whispered.

He took her in his arms lightly as if she were some fragile, precious thing. He kissed her tenderly, then turned abruptly and walked away.

D'oro closed the door quietly behind her and leaned against it for support while she attempted to gain control of her surging emotions. She could hear the receding sound of Bret's low melodious whistle as he walked back to the car. Her hearing alert to his every movement, she heard him return the quiet Porsche to the garage. Then she heard the noisier engine of his pickup as he gunned it down the road in a burst of exuberance not at all characteristic of his driving. There had been no doubt between them that she had accepted an invitation to more than dinner.

Chapter Ten

D'oro was awakened by the intrusion of sunlight
reaching persistently beneath the bottom of the
shuttered drapes. She had not expected to sleep at
all when she crept forlornly between the cool
sheets of the big mission bed. She had been
jumpy as a cat, charged with feelings of frustration, anticipation, doubt, and a pervading sense of
being alone in the rambling ranch house, which
had always before seemed so secure and hospita-
ble. Finally the combination of tired muscles, a
long day in the open air, and youthful hope for a
perfect new day had won for her the solace of
deep sleep. Yawning, she stretched in luxurious
lassitude, free of the demands of a work day. She
took a long, leisurely shower and shampooed and
blow-dried her hair, leaving it shining like golden
silk waving softly to frame her face. She fixed herself a brunch of fresh orange juice, Mexican
ranch-style eggs with crisp bacon, and toasted English muffins. When she had finished the brief
task of clearing away her breakfast things, she
could no longer postpone facing the reality that

she had merely delayed her departure by one day. She knew she was not yet ready to make a firm decision on her destination, so she had temporized by planning to spend a few days in San Francisco, a city she had often read about with eager interest. Whatever her destination, the necessity remained to pack. D'oro set about the job with grim determination, leaving out only her riding clothes for a last farewell trek with Bonanza and the outfit she intended to wear for dinner with Bret. The thought of their rendezvous filled her with tingling excitement that did not quite mask vague feelings of misgiving.

By midafternoon she was ready to go to the laboratory to complete the final task she had set for herself. She decided she would work in the blue slacks and coordinated print top she was wearing, and then change in the laboratory when she was finished.

At the fork in the road to the mine D'oro bypassed the turnoff she usually took to a parking spot in the trees. She chose instead the road that led directly to Bret's trailer, so that she would not have to walk back through the dark woods after dinner. She was disappointed to find that Bret's pickup was not in its accustomed spot when she parked beside the neatly laid-out path to his door.

She walked the short distance to the laboratory with the disturbing sensation that something was different. The little ore car stood idle below the chute from the mine. As her eyes followed the track for the car out to the ore dump, she froze with shock and anger. The entire stockpile of ore had been hauled away the previous day while they were at Yosemite! Bret had deliberately used the trip to conceal from her the fact that he had given up all hope of her supplying the formula needed to mill his own ore. He had made the decision long enough ago to make all the necessary arrangements for shipment of his ore to the smelter.

She felt crushed and humiliated that he had so little confidence in her ability, and worse, he had been right. That was what had occupied his time away from the mine since the day he took her down in the tunnel. At least he hadn't been with Candy, said the jealous little part of her emotions that concerned itself only with her personal relations. She could not help feeling patronized, like a child who had had a failure and was being urged by an adult to keep her chin up. She felt a strong desire just to turn and run away from the whole frustrating situation, but that would complete her admission of incompetence. She could at least finish her work in a professional manner by preparing a precise report of her experiments for her employer.

Squaring her shoulders determinedly, she unlocked the laboratory and hung her skirt and blouse on a nail at one side of the door. Her enthusiasm for the planned dinner had evaporated. One thing at a time, she thought grimly as she marched to the typewriter on a small table in one corner of the laboratoy.

Protruding from the carriage of the typewriter was a generous check for her work at the laboratory. She jerked it from the roller with fingers that itched to simply tear it up. Her work had been a failure. She had accomplished nothing, but not to accept payment for her work would be emotional, not professional, she realized. With reluctance she put the check in her purse. She recognized that it was evidence of Bret's tact and attention to detail that he had chosen to make payment that way rather than allowing the matter of money to intrude on their dinner, if in fact there was to be a dinner.

With determined discipline she inserted paper in the typewriter, placed the spectrographic analysis on the desk beside it, and began a concise report of each of the alphabetized elements in the ore with which she had worked. She was as far as manganese when she heard Bret's pickup. Glancing at her watch, she saw that it was four thirty. At least her timing had been right. She could finish the report with plenty of time to freshen up.

When she first discovered the missing stockpile of ore and knew the reason behind Bret's invitation, she had considered finishing her work and leaving without facing Bret's hypocrisy again. But she had delayed too long making a decision. With her car still parked beside his front door she couldn't very well walk over to it and calmly drive away.

When the report reached zinc and the final failure of the formula to react to the addition of zinc pellets, D'oro added her signature, stacked the pages neatly beside the typewriter, and weighted them with a gleaming sample of the ore.

With mounting eagerness that was in sharp contrast to the picture she planned to present, D'oro changed for her dinner date. She had selected a floor-length skirt of frosted blue hand-woven Mexican cotton with floral embroidery connected by a tracery of silver thread. With it she wore an off-the-shoulder fiesta blouse of lace-edged white voile. The blouse was the perfect companion for the delicate silver filigree butterfly pendant Bret had bought her at Yosemite. Fortunately, her evening sandals had been selected to match the silver tracery of her skirt. Her outfit seemed a little formal for dinner in a trailer, but fiesta was not a place or a time of day, she knew. It was a feeling of dancing and happiness in the heart, and her heart was certainly pounding to a flamenco beat as she put the final touches on her light makeup.

Gathering her work clothes in her arms, she deposited them in her car, then turned toward Bret's door. Since the first bantered exchange about her sharing his trailer on the day she arrived, she had not received an invitation to her employer's domain until then.

The door was open, and she could see Thor watching her approach through the screen. When she started up the steps, the dog put one paw on the catch, opening the door for her. He continued to hold the paw elevated in the traditional gesture of a dog offering to shake hands.

Solemnly D'oro accepted the invitation, adding in the spirit of the game, "It's good to see you again."

Bret's deep appreciative laugh sounding from the shadows behind the dog melted the tension that had been building all day, like sun breaking through morning fog.

She had seen magazine advertisements for mobile living quarters such as she found herself in, but she had never been in a luxury-built mobile home. The living room was spacious with wood paneling and picture windows and had obviously been decorated by a professional. The leather upholstered furniture and heavy mission oak tables were masculine, yet homelike. Colorful Indian rugs added contrast and western character to the decor. She had never suspected that Bret lived in such opulence at his mine, though it was certainly in character.

"With the shortage of help, Thor has to double as butler," Bret said lightly as he held out his hands to her while his intense blue eyes registered approval of the way she looked in her fiesta dress.

As she extended her hands to meet his, they both noticed that her hand was dusty from shaking Thor's paw.

"Never could train him to wear white gloves," Bret joked. "The bathroom is down the hall if you'd like to wash your hands."

D'oro smiled with delight when she entered the room Bret indicated. In the bathroom Bret had indulged his fondness for anything silver in a manner so lavish, he seemed also to be laughing at himself. The color scheme was completely white and silver. A large sunken bathtub with massive chrome fittings was totally surrounded by mirrors. The paper on the walls of the room was white with insets of silver foil cut in diamond shape. The vanity table was topped with mirror-tile, and a large mirror backed the basin and vanity. D'oro found herself reflected from every conceivable angle. It suddenly reminded her of Sally's bathroom at Zacatecas. She had never liked all the mirrors, as such preening self-admiration embarrassed her. Then she noticed that the bright foil diamonds in the wallpaper produced a small distorted image that would drive her mother or Candy crazy. She laughed at the idea, which she suspected was deliberate. Away from business she had often enjoyed Bret's sharp sense of humor. She washed her hands and dried them on one of the neatly stacked guest towels. The gentleman certainly was attentive to details.

As she returned to the hall D'oro's eye was caught by the room at the opposite end from where she had been. In front of the open door was a king-size water bed spread with a silver velveteen throw. D'oro could just picture Candy stretching luxuriously like a great white cat with her silver-blond hair fanning out around her in a sensuous pose.

"Ever try a water bed?" Bret asked so close behind her that she jumped with surprise. The thick carpeting had muffled his approaching footsteps.

It was a no-win question, and they both knew it. She did not want to say no and seem like a naive schoolgirl as she had on their first ride, when she had hesitated about responding to the intimacy of his kiss, but she was not willing to claim experience she had not had. She shook her head.

"Mighty restful," he continued with a smirk

that brought a flood of color to D'oro's face. As she lowered her eyes she could feel him continue to study her face as if searching for something. He led the way to the living room and seated her on a love seat in front of a large picture window that framed the pine-covered mountains against the fading daylight. From the built-in bar he brought frosty margaritas. As she sipped the cool drink tangy with fresh lime and the salt in which the rim of the glass was rubbed, she wondered at his insight in selecting her favorite Mexican drink. Her father always served margaritas at what he called his "thank-you-note suppers," to which he invited the charming relatives and friends of company officials he was asked to escort to dinner parties or fiestas when they visited Zacatecas. The thought that Bret was like her father when he was younger made D'oro feel like an immature daddy's girl.

"To our delightful imports from Mexico," Bret toasted.

She thought she had never seen his eyes so startlingly blue. "Tell me about your home in Zacatecas," he said as if he knew it was in her thoughts.

"Our hacienda is similar to Annie's," she replied, then hesitated as thoughts came flooding back to her of the troubled past in which her father and Annie had been involved.

"Do you keep horses?" he cut in smoothly as if sensing he had touched on a subject that disturbed her.

"Only two—mine and one for whoever is available to ride with me."

"Your father doesn't ride?"

"He says he's a Johnny-come-lately, not raised to it. I guess that's why I have had a pony since I was big enough to stay on one. He said being an accomplished horsewoman was a tradition among great ladies." As she repeated her father's words she wondered if they were in some way connected with Annie. In her present state of mind she seemed to be looking for such connections where they might not exist at all.

"Your horsemanship seems to pass the test," he said, grinning at the memory of the race in which she had beaten him.

D'oro flushed at the reminder. "The lessons came later at boarding school. One of their many desperate attempts to make a proper senorita of the independent little Yankee."

"Instead you became a mad scientist mixing magic potions in a test tube," he teased. Though his tone was light, there seemed to be unasked questions behind the entire conversation about her past. She hoped it was only that he was as eager to know everything about her as she was about him. He smiled at her then, and she felt its warmth suffuse her whole being. Their eyes met and held, then he abruptly turned away.

He crossed to the stereo and changed the tape from the light classical music that had been playing softly in the background to a sensuous Latin serenade by Laurindo Almeida. Its tempo matched the mounting excitement she felt in the intimacy of his home.

"Guess it's time to see what kind of grub this

sourdough can dish up," he said, mimicking the old miners they had met at Coulterville.

The table in the dinette was covered with a handwoven linen cloth and set with earth-tone pottery. Colorful zinnias filled a Mexican pottery bowl. When he opened the oven, the tantalizing aroma of beef Stroganoff filled the room. Mingling with it came the smell of heated French bread.

Everything from the crispness of the green salad to the spicy creaminess of the Stroganoff sauce was perfect as she knew it would be. Just as she knew Bret's lovemaking would be perfect in every detail. D'oro hastily put that thought from her mind. She took a deep breath and tried to calm her tension enough to eat the delicious meal he had prepared for her.

The room seemed filled with Bret's presence, alive with his magnetism, until D'oro had trouble concentrating on their conversation about their interest in Thor and the horses and early-day mining lore. She found pleasure in the insight his words gave into his complex thoughts and moods, but she was confused by his deliberate casualness.

"The dinner was perfect," she said, sipping the rich mellow wine, which reflected the candlelight in a ruby glow on her fingertips.

"The inspiration was right," he said with a huskiness that had not been in his voice before. When she set her glass down, his hand covered hers. He pulled out her chair for her, his lips brushing the back of her neck as she rose. In spite of the mounting excitement in her, she eluded the lure of his arms until the simple tasks of putting his efficient, dishwasher-equipped kitchen in order were completed and Thor had been duly rewarded with his share of the delicious meal. There was an intimacy about sharing the simple household tasks in his home that D'oro found reassuring.

The stage was set to perfection when they were again settled on the love seat with a backdrop of shadowed mountains above which a silvery moon hung suspended. The stereo was playing soft pulsating rhythms, the lights were low, and two tiny glasses of Mexican orange liqueur sat on the end table beside them. His arms around her shoulders tightened, drawing her to him in an embrace so close, she could scarcely breathe. His lips came down on her expectant mouth in the kiss she had been dreaming of all day. A familiar surge of pleasure went through her when his lips touched hers. His mouth was not gentle and caressing as it had been the previous day, it was hard and bruising. Impatiently his thrusting tongue parted her lips, bringing desire in a sudden rush of passion far different from the slowly building awareness he had coaxed from her by the lake.

D'oro's fingers played along the crisp curly hair at his temples before sliding behind his handsome head. His arms locked around her waist in a vise-like grip. He leaned back along the couch, carrying her with him so that her weight pressed her soft body close against his lean hard length. She started to laugh at his maneuver, but when she looked in his eyes there was no merriment there, only a strange hooded expression she had not seen before.

Bret's lips trailed searing kisses down her throat, then traced the rounded fullness of her breasts, half-exposed by her new position. His hands explored her body with calculated boldness, causing fire to race through her veins and pound in tempo with the flamenco rhythm that flooded from the stereo, ever louder and more insistent.

Her temples throbbed with the pounding of her blood, which he was setting afire with such practiced certainty. The sensation of allowing him to direct the reaction of her body frightened her. It was like a perverse attempt to keep her knee from kicking when the doctor tested her reflexes with his little hammer. Well, her reflexes were working just fine. She was determined not to allow her inexperience to again become a barrier between them.

Touching his cheek with her lips, she traced its taut outline with soft little kisses. For a moment he hesitated, then relaxed and smiled at her in his heartstopping way. A glow of happiness joined the rush of desire he had aroused in her. She loved him so much.

When his lips caught hers, there was the gentleness she found so endearing, but immediately the harsh demands began again, clearly foreshadowing his expectations. Something was wrong. There was no tenderness, no gentle teasing to coax her senses and her affection. His every movement was harsh, abrasive, calculated. On the previous day he had looked into her eyes as if trying to probe their depths, but now he seemed to be avoiding them. Having won her acquiescence, did he no longer feel the need to pretend affection for her? She had come seeking a shared moment to cherish wherever she went, not a tawdry one-night stand.

D'oro slid her hands from around his neck and braced them against his shoulders, pushing away from him. Her strength was no match for his, and he only laughed with a low sensuous rumble as if it were a game. His lips trailed a path of burning sensitivity along the line of her scoop-necked blouse, pausing to raise tingling excitement at the cleavage between her breasts.

Struggling against her own desires as much as his superior strength, she kicked and squirmed and twisted. The commotion brought Thor bounding into the living room. The sight of his two favorite people locked in a struggle made the dog frantic with indecision as to which one to protect. He charged, retreated, and barked commands reinforced with throaty growls. Bret released his hold, and D'oro sprang to her feet.

"It's all right, boy. She had me fooled, too," he soothed the dog in a voice filled with bitterness and irony and frustrated passion.

"What made you think I would be another of your easy conquests?" she lashed out.

"Isn't that part of a spy's repertoire?" he sneered, his anger matching hers.

"And what am I supposed to be spying on? You're the one who wanted someone to bring you the Rodriguez formula."

"That you conveniently forgot—if you ever knew it, which I doubt."

D'oro snatched up her purse and whirled toward the door, but Bret's hand shot out and clamped around her wrist.

"Take your father a message for me. Tell him I almost fell for your wide-eyed innocent act. If I hadn't gone to the mine recorder's office today to get an ownership certificate for my ore shipment tomorrow, you'd have been gone before I found out."

"Found out what?"

"That he sent you here to get information about the new strike I made in the Heartbreaker and to find out whether it runs through to the Silver Queen."

"My father is in South America. He doesn't even know I'm here."

"So you decided to launch out on your own after he gave you his half of the Silver Queen? Like father, like daughter, except that a woman doesn't have to kill the opponent like he did Annie's husband. A woman has other ways of getting information from a man."

D'oro's free hand lashed out at his arrogant face, set in a mirthless triumphant smile, but he kept her at arm's length, and she struck empty air.

"The jury acquitted him of the murder!" she shouted.

"That's what I kept telling myself. But what would you expect when a popular local man kills an outsider whom nobody liked? If he was so innocent, why did he go running off to Mexico?"

D'oro felt the unreasoning hurt and bewilderment of a child defending a parent in a schoolyard fight when the taunts of the detractor echoed her own doubts. Wrapping the strap of her shoulder bag around her free hand, she swung it at Bret's head. That was too much for Thor. His ingrained instincts told him where his loyalties were. With a low growl he sprang for D'oro's throat.

Bret's movements were as quick and instinctive as the dog's. Releasing D'oro's wrist, he caught both powerful hands in the dog's collar and fur, literally wrestling the agitated dog to the floor.

D'oro turned and fled to her waiting car, seeing the way only dimly through the flood of her tears.

Chapter Eleven

D'oro unlocked the massive oak door of the ranch house and all but collapsed inside. She was not sure how she had gotten there except that the road from the mine was so familiar, her every movement was automatic. She stumbled to her room, glad there was no one else in the house to make pretense necessary. She flung herself on the big old mission bed, her body racked with convulsive sobs.

Why had Bret's behavior suddenly changed toward her between their trip to Yosemite the previous day and that night at his trailer? she asked bitterly. In spite of the seriousness with which he did his work, he was just like other wealthy American playboys she had seen at the university in Mexico in the summer. Once he was certain of his conquest, he dropped all pretense of love. But why had he dragged her father and her own failure into it? He had known about the accident at the Silver Queen from the time he bought the Heartbreaker Mine. She felt certain he had been the one the clerk mentioned who had been reading the old issues of the *Mariposa Gazette,* so even those details published in the paper weren't new to him. To taunt her with the knowledge like that had been despicable. She had never believed that love and hate could be so closely bound up together. She felt drained and empty.

Sometime during the long miserable night D'oro heard Annie's horse van move down the road. A short time later she heard the staccato click of Annie's heels on the tile floor. She heard the footsteps approach her door, hesitate, then cross to Annie's own room. She was glad that Annie had decided not to disturb her. Telling the older woman of whom she had grown so fond of her decision to leave was going to be difficult in the morning. She hadn't the strength left to face it that night.

D'oro felt she would never sleep again, but the purging effect of tears proved to be a powerful tranquilizer. She slept fitfully, fighting with the horrors of a nightmare in which either her father or Bret in a confusion of identity were working down in a black pit of a mine. Then there was the crashing of the hoist. In the endless futility of a dream she clawed at the dirt with her bare hands, trying to rescue someone—her father, Bret, Annie, herself, she didn't know whom.

D'oro awakened early, feeling as tired and listless as if she hadn't slept at all. She lay staring at the heavy oak beams of the ceiling with no wish to return to the nightmare by trying to sleep again. Her eyes shifted to the window framing the soft morning light. She hadn't bothered to close the drapes the previous night. On a chair beside the window sat her open suitcase. Her fiesta skirt and blouse lay in a heap on top. She didn't care if she never saw them again, but to leave them behind would raise questions. Blinking, she turned her head away. In the otherwise empty closet she saw the reminder of the last thing she intended to do before she left Mariposa. She had left her riding clothes out for a last run on Bonanza.

D'oro rolled listlessly out of bed and decided to postpone her shower until she returned from her ride, lest the running water wake Annie. She hoped to say her farewells at the last minute. After dressing quickly, she gave her hair a perfunctory brush and slipped quietly out the patio door, carrying her boots to avoid the ring of her heels on the tile floor. The hand-tooled leather of her boots still had a new look about it, reminding her of her first ride with Bret, when the slick soles had dumped her at his feet and later caused her to slide down the hill into the crush of his arms. She was dismayed to find that the longing for him that should have been extinguished was still there. Love shouldn't hurt so much even when it was hopeless.

The slanting rays of the morning sun warmed her face but could not reach her heart as she stopped beside the kitchen door to put on her boots. When she neared the barn, she was surprised to find that both Rattlesnake and Annie were already there. Rattlesnake led a handsome coal-black horse out into the corral, patting his nose with special pride.

"Meet Megatite, our new champion two-year-old," said Annie. She smiled as she recalled how she had dashed from her taxi into the stands in time to see the horses going into the first turn with Megatite a length and a half behind the leader. Mike, her jockey, had timed his move perfectly, bringing her horse in first by half a length. Her trainer, Hank, and some of the others in the winner's circle who knew her well took a second look when she appeared wearing a dress rather than her accustomed pantsuit.

"You're looking a heap better," Hank had told her with a hint of suspicion in his voice.

Annie had been so anxious to get back to the ranch that she hadn't even stayed for the winner's celebration. She had been tempted to go to D'oro's room when she arrived, but she wasn't certain what to tell D'oro about her affair with Jim.

Annie watched D'oro pat the horse's nose and speak as much to him as to his owner. "Congratulations, Megatite. So, like the magnetic black sand you're named for, you've begun to collect the gold."

Annie smiled with pleasure, but the real treasure she had brought home from the weekend was not another winner's plaque. It was the memory of one perfect night of love, and the knowledge that Jim loved her, and always had. She understood, accepted the fact that there would be no marriage, no commitment between them. It was strange that it had never occurred to her how an honorable man like Jim would feel about the accident. She could still cling to the hope that somewhere, sometime fate and his conscience would allow her another few hours of bliss in his arms. With a sigh she mounted gracefully into the racing saddle that Rattlesnake had put on Megatite instead of the usual silver-mounted western saddle. It was a comfortable life if a lonely one that she had built for herself, but since it had the tiniest spark of hope in it, she knew it would once again hold sharp pain and anguished thoughts of what might have been.

Megatite pranced around the corral, his head held high, his neck arched, as if he fully understood his victory. Annie rode with the good seat, hands, posture, and control of a horse show champion. Watching, D'oro remembered her father's comments about horsemanship being one of the accomplishments of a great lady.

Rattlesnake reappeared, leading Bonanza. As D'oro patted the beloved horse before mounting she murmured to him in the way of animal lovers who can't resist talking to their favorites. "I wouldn't trade you for all the champions."

"Wouldn't need to. Bonanza won more races than any other horse in my stable in his younger days," said Annie, smiling. D'oro blushed in confusion when she realized she had been talking aloud to her horse.

"I didn't expect you out so early," D'oro said when Rattlesnake had let them out the corral gate.

"Wanted to give Megatite a little workout this morning after his ride in the van yesterday, and I have an appointment later in the morning." Annie turned toward the foothills as Bret had on D'oro's first ride. When they reached the open meadow, Annie's horse broke into a run, but Bonanza wasn't taken by surprise as Bret's horse had been. With a burst of speed the old veteran overtook the two-year-old and maintained the lead for half the width of the meadow before the new champion's conditioning and Annie's professional handling gave the victory to Megatite.

With her usually carefully groomed hair tumbling around her face and her throaty laughter ringing in the air, Annie seemed scarcely older than D'oro. "Thought for a minute Bonanza was going to put this youngster in his place."

"I've never known a horse like Bonanza before," answered D'oro, her eyes sparkling briefly before the dull hurt look returned.

In companionable silence they rode to the top of the lower ridge and looked back down the valley where the perfect symmetry and proportions of the ranch house were then visible through the leafless silhouette of the hardwood trees. D'oro recalled with a feeling of loss the brilliant fall foliage that had filled the valley the first time she had ridden there with Bret.

"When will you be leaving?' Annie asked in a carefully controlled voice. As soon as she had entered the house the night before she had been aware that everything belonging to D'oro had been carefully collected.

D'oro gave the other woman a quick surprised look and then, avoiding her eyes, answered, "As soon as possible after our ride."

"Is your work finished, then?"

"As much as I can do. It was a failure." D'oro's voice was as flat and listless as her eyes.

"I'm sorry." The words seemed so inadequate. Annie thought it might be some consolation for D'oro to know that the process had not worked on that particular ore for Juan, either. However, telling her about that part of her trip would mean admitting that she had anticipated D'oro's failure. She felt sure that Juan would continue to work on the puzzling problem. It was possible he would find a quick solution and that Jim would let her know, but she wasn't sure that would be any great help between D'oro and Bret. Instinctively she knew that he was the cause of the pain that was reflected in everything D'oro said or did. Annie wanted desperately to find some way to help Jim's daughter, who had become so closely identified with her own lost youth, but there seemed to be nothing she could do.

"Where will you go?"

"San Francisco for a few days. I've always wanted to see it. After that I haven't decided yet."

Annie knew that she would have to let D'oro know that Jim was back from South America and anxious for her to go home if that was a choice D'oro wished to make. She took a deep breath and set her shoulders in a characteristic gesture. She would have to tell D'oro everything, but first she wanted to talk to Bret, find out just what the situation was with him. "I have to go back now for my appointment. It shouldn't take long. Will you wait until I get back?"

D'oro hesitated.

"Please."

D'oro nodded. It was only a few hours drive to San Francisco, and it seemed important to Annie that they not say good-bye there.

"If you're riding over to the Silver Queen, don't let Bonanza drink from the pool at the base of the old ore pile. There's a lot of arsenic in that ore, which overflows into the pool when it rains."

D'oro was startled that Annie had guessed even before the thought was fully formed in her own mind that she had to see the Silver Queen for herself before she left Mariposa forever. She cut across the autumn-brown hills in the familiar direction of the Heartbreaker Mine and its ill-famed neighbor, the Silver Queen. She did not take the new road that Bret used to the Heartbreaker, though from what he had said the night before about the ownership certificate for his shipment, she was sure he would already be gone. About half a mile beyond the familiar road she found traces of an old road running in the same general direction and she followed it.

When D'oro emerged from the pines at the crest of the hill and entered the clearing, she could scarcely believe her eyes. The hoist house and scaffolding were in perfect repair and recently painted. The forest had not been allowed to encroach on the claim.

She dismounted and tied Bonanza at the corner of the hoist house. As she passed the window she could see that the machinery was encased in protective grease. It was as if all were being kept in readiness for the return of the miner. D'oro recalled that Annie had mentioned when she arrived that she might reopen the Silver Queen or lease it if Bret set up a mill. During their fight Bret seemed to imply that her father owned part of the Silver Queen, but that couldn't be true. D'oro was certain there had been no contact between Annie and her father since the family moved to Mexico. It would surely have been necessary if they were partners. The thought of Bret and the terrible, angry, hurting things he said brought tears of despair to her eyes. *He isn't worth it,* she told herself severely, recalling with burning shame that his lovemaking had held nothing more than skillful seduction. He was worse than the most macho Latin males she had scorned at the university who seemed interested only in easy conquest.

"I despise him!" she told the startled Bonanza, but something deep inside her seemed to disagree.

As if dragged along by them, D'oro followed the slack cables from the hoist house to the mine entrance. A gasp of horror escaped her as she peered down the murky shaft. Halfway down there was a jumble of broken cable beside a great black hole where the side of the shaft had been torn away. She could not see the bottom of the shaft where her mind told her the debris had landed. It was an eerie, ghost-filled sensation as the newspaper account of the accident took form before her eyes.

D'oro stumbled from the mine entrance back to the comforting presence of her patiently waiting horse. She loosed the tether and mounted quickly, as if expecting pursuing demons. She did not head back in the direction from which she had come, but turned in the direction of the old ore pile, which seemed not to have been picked over or disturbed since the day of the accident.

At the end of the pile Bonanza hesitated and turned his head expectantly toward a small stream-fed pool. Immediately Annie's words came back to her: *"Don't let Bonanza drink from the pool at the base of the old ore pile. There's a lot of arsenic in that ore. . . ."*

D'oro could see that the ground surrounding the pool was covered with a fine white powder where the high spring water had evaporated. Her experience confirmed the likelihood that it was arsenic. Of the substances she had analyzed in organic chemistry class, arsenic stood out in her mind above all the others. One of the boys in her class, looking for a shortcut around all the testing, had tasted the white powder they were supposed to analyze. That easy solution had worked for him on the previous substance, which had been salt, but that time his laziness landed him in the hospital with severe stomach cramps. D'oro smiled at the memory.

She turned her head from the pond to the ore pile. The chunks of gleaming white quartz were very like those from the Heartbreaker a few hundred yards away, except they were covered with the fine white powder from years of leaching in the rain. The spectrograph had not indicated the presence of arsenic in the ore, and she had made no tests for it. The arsenic could have thrown her formula off.

D'oro dismounted and tied Bonanza to a tree well away from the contaminated pool. She took a tissue from her pocket and scooped up a generous sample of the white powder. She was certain she knew all the properties of arsenic after her dramatic introduction to it, but she would not need to rely on her memory. Bret's laboratory contained an excellent set of chemistry reference books. As her lazy lab partner had known, results could be quick and easy if you knew in advance the substance you were working with. In minutes she could confirm that the powder was arsenic—without tasting it, she thought wryly.

She had already checked the other elements in the ore twice with the same results. If the sample proved to be arsenic and she could find in the manuals the way to neutralize it, she felt confident the formula would work.

D'oro shuddered at the thought of going back to the laboratory after the agony of the previous night's fight with Bret. Why should she after the things he said about her and her work? But she knew nothing would give her greater satisfaction than proving to the arrogant Bret Johnson that she could do what she said she could. It would be a fine piece of irony for him to get back from taking his ore to the smelter to find the formula he could have used to build his own mill. She squared her shoulders and lifted her small defiant chin in the air, ignoring the fact that her hands were trembling.

Undecided whether to ride Bonanza back to the ranch and drive to the laboratory or simply to ride the short distance between the two mines, D'oro walked over to where her horse was tied. As she loosened the reins she could see through the trees a small spring that would be safely free of contamination from the mine. She led Bonanza to the spring for a drink and was surprised to find that she could see the outline of Bret's trailer on the far side of the trees. She had not realized that the two mines were so close together.

Apparently recognizing her scent, Thor came bounding through the trees to meet her. Suddenly the dog froze as if remembering the previous night's altercation. As D'oro waited tensely for the dog's reaction he lowered his head and tail sheepishly and came forward to nuzzle her hand as if in apology. "You have better manners than your master," she reassured him, patting the dog's handsome head.

Thor's appearance settled her indecision. She found a patch of grass and shade where she could tie Bonanza, taking off the saddle and throwing it over the limb of a tree. She followed Thor back to the Heartbreaker. When she reached the clearing, she saw that Bret's pickup was still parked beside his trailer and she almost lost her resolution to complete her work.

Thor had run ahead of her and was lying beside the bandanna tied to the cable running into the mine. D'oro knew that it meant Bret was working down in the tunnel. Confirming her thinking, the ore bucket came climbing out of the shaft and noisily dumped its contents into the small ore car, which then ran out to the end of the track and dumped its contents where the ore pile had been.

D'oro was puzzled by Bret's change of plans when the rest of the ore had already been hauled to the railroad. The railroad car probably wasn't quite full, D'oro decided. If he paid a flat rate for the shipment, it would be good business to come back for what he needed. Since he was in a hurry, he probably wouldn't take time out for lunch. If she worked quickly, she should be finished and gone before Bret came up from his work.

Grateful that there was an extra key to the laboratory in the hoist house, which was open with the hoist running, D'oro went to work quickly and efficiently. Chemical tests confirmed that the white powder was arsenic. She selected a promising sample from the ore bucket and crushed it, and her tests revealed that there was arsenic present, as she was sure they would. While she considered the results of the tests the lifting and dumping process was repeated outside. It seemed to her there was less time between loads than usual. Bret must have been working very rapidly. It was almost as if it were a race between them to be finished first. The thought of Bret working in the mine with his miners' lamp casting shadows across his rugged features, and his plaid shirt straining across his broad shoulders, made her pulse pound and her breath quicken. She would not allow herself to think about the perfect communication that had seemed to exist between them the day he took her down into the mine.

The ore bucket dropping back down the shaft reminded her that she simply could not face Bret again. She set to work with grim determination. She dumped the crushed sample into a nitrate bath to remove the arsenic and began preparing the suspension solution. When the mixture was ready, she dropped the pretreated crushed ore into the flask and watched as the separation took place when it was retorted. Everything went just the way it had in Juan's laboratory, but it had done so there the first two times, up to the final step. The ore bucket had gone through its clattering dumping routine and returned down the shaft, where a bobbing motion of the cable indicated it was being filled again.

With a rush D'oro measured out the zinc pellets and added them to the murky mixture. She watched them filter slowly to the bottom of the flask. Then Juan's miracle occurred. The pellets were followed by a shower of tiny sparkling particles of gold and silver that nestled like metallic snow around the larger zinc pellets. She had done it!

The elation she had expected from success did not follow. Hastily she set the flask in a rack in the center of the workbench, clearing away everything else she had used in her experiment. She quickly typed a footnote to her report, which was still lying beside the typewriter, detailing the bath necessary to remove the arsenic from the ore. She assembled the report neatly and placed it on the workbench beside the flask, weighting it with a choice specimen of ore. She would let Annie know of her success in case Bret did not find occasion to use the laboratory when he returned from the smelter.

With a feeling that she had won the battle but lost the war, D'oro picked up her purse and closed and locked the laboratory door behind her. She was replacing the key on its hook in the hoist house when the loud jangling of the phone behind her startled her, so that she dropped the key. She took the time to retrieve the key and hang it up, allowing the phone to ring a second and a third time. It was probably Candy, she guessed, tempted not to answer at all.

D'oro had never been able to resist a ringing telephone, so after the third ring she picked it up and answered, "Heartbreaker Mine," as businesslike as possible.

"D'oro, glad to find you there," rasped Rattlesnake's Texas twang.

"Rattlesnake! Is something wrong?"

"It's Annie. When she got home from town, she found that Megatite was a little stiff from the race and the trailer ride. She took him out for another workout, and he threw her."

"How bad is she hurt?"

"She's unconscious. Looks like a concussion. Doc hasn't had time to check for breaks or internal injury."

"I'll be there as quick as I can ride back—"

"Uh, honey, is Bret there?" Rattlesnake interrupted hesitantly.

"Yes..." D'oro answered with equal hesitation.

"Annie has been calling for him in her delirium. Could you let him know?"

"Of course." The phone clicked dead, but D'oro stood holding it a moment, lost in a torrent of conflicting emotions. Her mind shrieked in dismay at having to face Bret again, but somewhere inside of her a pulse surged with hope at seeing him one more time before she left.

So there was more between them than friendship, just as D'oro had suspected when she learned Bret had given Annie the Porsche. And Annie wanted him, needed him then. But how was she to let him know? There was no communication between the tunnel and anyone above ground. He might finish what he was doing and ascend at any time.

Even as she pondered the problem the ore car went through its automatic routine. Like Thor, she watched the bandanna hopefully for indication that Bret would be on his way up. The intermittent motion that indicated the bucket was being refilled began again. He would be at least half an hour, and might work until five o'clock or even longer if he was trying to get a precise quantity of ore to complete the shipment.

D'oro couldn't chance waiting. She would have to go down and tell him. It wasn't that big a deal, she had done it before. Unfortunately, the heavy clothing she had worn the first time was in the back of her VW at the ranch, but her riding breeches and boots were good and sturdy. She looked around the hoist house and found an old plaid wool shirt of Bret's to put over her light cotton blouse. The elusive woodsy smell of his after-shave lotion still clung to the collar of his shirt, filling her with excitement and the courage to go down into the mine after him.

The extra hard hat with a miners' lamp on it hung on a peg. She attached the battery to her belt, adjusted the hat, and tried the beam. It worked without problems. Feeling like a little girl playing dress-up in the oversize shirt and hat, D'oro hurried to the portal of the mine. Thor trotted over to her, then made an agitated trip to the bandanna, then back to her. He was obviously disturbed by the unusual sequence of events, so she stopped to pat the beautiful animal and talk to him reassuringly before starting down the ladder.

Without the reassuring presence of Bret beneath her on the ladder, D'oro experienced misgivings about the project. Then she thought of Annie and the strong bond that had developed between them. Annie needed Bret, and she would get him, D'oro resolved as she gripped the side rails of the ladder tightly and began moving down the rungs. By the time she reached the first platform she felt more confident. Below the second level she came to the solid rock portion of the shaft, which she remembered, and below that the moist dripping of ground seepage. She paused to rest at the tenth level beside the open drift Bret had mentioned. She counted the rungs as she descended, watched for different color patterns in the quartz, anything to distract her mind from the memory of the day she went down in the mine with Bret. As she neared the bottom the memory of missing his sneak-thief step and being caught in Bret's strong arms was so vivid that she could almost feel his presence. She extended her leg for an unusually long step and her foot touched solid rock. She turned her headlamp around the perimeter of the shaft. The beam rested briefly on the large pulley through which the hoist cable operated. She thought of the mess of tangled hoist cable in the Silver Queen and a shudder ran through her. She hadn't noticed the pulley on her first trip down in the mine, but held in Bret's arms, she hadn't had eyes for such prosaic things.

D'oro stared with apprehension at the gaping entry of the inky black tunnel and hesitated, but the thought that Bret was somewhere in that tunnel and that she must find him for Annie gave her a two-pronged reason to proceed. Ducking her head as Bret had instructed her to avoid low overhang focused the beam of D'oro's miners' lamp on the floor of the tunnel in front of her giving her some reassurance. Still, it was a far different experience creeping through the dark tunnel than it had been following Bret's broad comforting back. She turned once to look back down the tunnel in the direction from which she had come. The dim light from the shaft had become a tiny circle. It hadn't seemed nearly so far the first time as it did while she was alone.

With her head down D'oro almost ran into the end of the tunnel before she realized she was there. But where was Bret? It had never occurred to her that she might not find him. She focused her light on the solid rock blocking the tunnel.

She reached out her hand and felt the rough texture of the surface as she had before. There was no doubt that was the end of the tunnel. Fighting mounting panic, she sat down on the solid rock of the floor of the tunnel and leaned back against the wall of rock that marked its end. She closed her eyes, trying to think, and leaned her head and shoulders heavily against the rock behind her to ease the cramp of her stooped walking position.

Suddenly she felt herself sliding, falling, tumbling backward. The rock had given way! She screamed Bret's name again and again while the walls flung her voice back at her in mocking echo. It was the sound of the echo that finally caused her to stop and listen for an answer from the inky blackness that surrounded her. She had lost her hat and light in the fall. The quiet act of listening brought a return of rationality. She cautiously flexed her hands and feet to see that all operated without damage. Her hips and shoulders felt bruised, though she did not seem to have fallen very far. It had been like falling down a coal chute. Certainly no coal bin was ever blacker than the impenetrable darkness in which D'oro found herself. If only she had some light! She didn't even carry matches, but she automatically searched her pants pockets. When her hand touched the wool shirt, she remembered that she was wearing Bret's shirt, but he didn't smoke, either. Though her mind said there wouldn't be any, her fingers searched the shirt pockets and clutched a slender packet of matches as if they were a lifeline to her sanity. Of course, it was a work shirt, and he had matches to light dynamite fuses. She found it was surprisingly difficult to light matches in total darkness. She finally scratched the head of one across the striker, producing a spark, then a feeble flickering flame. It showed nothing except the rock on which she was sitting. She lit a second match before the flame of the first quite reached her fingers. That time the flame reflected back from her hard hat, and a third match enabled her to crawl to the spot where it lay. Hoarding the precious matches as much as possible, D'oro worked in darkness to pick up the hat and follow along the cord to the battery. With both of them in her hands, she thumped at the light and manipulated the switch until she was rewarded with a beam of light.

She gasped in confusion to find that she was in a tiny room hewed out of the rock. Just beyond her reach was a pile of army blankets, old and musty. Beside them was a large canteen and a stack of small mildewing white boxes. Cautiously she opened one of the boxes to find that it was neatly packed with olive drab cans labeled fruit cocktail, chopped ham, crackers. A mustiness hung over everything. There were decomposed packets that seemed to have contained seasonings and powdered coffee. The upper box had protected the printing on the lid of the box beneath it: "C rations—use before December 1960."

Those things had been brought to the room more than twenty years ago. But why? A bomb shelter? Hardly that deep in the shaft or that far along the tunnel. A hideout? But who and why?

D'oro knew very little of the history of the Heartbreaker Mine, but no one had ever mentioned any mystery or trouble connected with the Heartbreaker. Yet, if it were the Silver Queen... Just the name caused an uneasiness in the pit of D'oro's stomach. Had she been going in the direction of the Silver Queen? Could there be any possible connection? Could someone from the Silver Queen have hidden out here? Certainly not her father. The sheriff had been keeping track of his whereabouts.

A sickening thought began to take shape in D'oro's mind. Clay Nalton's body was never recovered. Could Clay Nalton have hidden out here while her father was being tried for his murder? D'oro's flesh crawled with a perception of evil more frightening than even the darkness had been.

Her lamp made menacing shadows along the walls as she looked around the tiny room. It was nearly round. The ceiling and most of the walls were solid quartz. Behind the blankets was a break in the solid rock that might have been an opening filled with chunks of broken rock. Could this room be connected to the Silver Queen, providing an underground passage from one mine to the other? D'oro turned to examine the wall in the direction from which she had come.

Just above the level of her head rusted dirt-caked hinges and a spring were bolted to a rock that was marked by a definite crack all the way around. It looked almost like heavy-duty screen door hardware. A rusty bolt protruded from the lower corner. She grasped the bolt with trembling hands and pulled. Nothing happened. She braced her feet against the wall, took a firmer hold on the bolt, and threw her weight against it. She was rewarded by the sound of rock grating on rock and a slight movement of the stone door. She made a second effort, but the rusted bolt snapped off in her hands. Free of her weight, the spring pushed the stone back into its original position. She stood staring hopelessly at a heavy stone trapdoor with no handle to open it from the inside. In frustration D'oro beat on it with her fists. When exhaustion overcame her from the physical exertion of kicking, pounding, and yelling, her mind began to take command of the situation again.

As though performing an experiment in the laboratory, she began to analyze her problem. It was hard to think clearly about the emotions and events that had brought her down into the mine. There had never been a woman in her life to whom she felt as close as Annie, and the older woman seemed to feel the same about her. According to Rattlesnake, Annie had been in love with D'oro's father. She sometimes wondered if she still was. She had no idea how her father felt about Annie, only that he had shied away from commitment to any other woman since Sally left. D'oro wasn't sure how Bret fit into the picture. She sometimes got the impression that Bret and Annie had once been lovers, but that no longer appeared to be true. Perhaps it was the similarity between Bret and her father that D'oro herself had often noticed. Whatever their relationship,

Annie was hurt and in need of Bret's strength and comfort. Somehow in trying to get that message to him, D'oro had not felt the jealous torment of giving him over to another woman. The whole thing was terribly mixed up and confusing.

D'oro was sure her bitter conflicting feelings about Bret had been the distraction that put her in the spot she was in. She had made a mistake somewhere and gone in the wrong direction, or she was on the wrong level of the mine. She had fallen through a sort of trapdoor into an old shelter or hideout, apparently unused for twenty years. Superstition, which had seeped into her thinking during her younger years in Mexico, kept whispering that she had been drawn to the room by evil forces. The logical part of her mind rejected the idea. She was prevented from escaping from the hideout by a solid stone door held in place by a heavy spring, a door that no longer had a handle or any other device for opening it from the inside. She felt like a child who had gotten shut inside an unused refrigerator, except that the room wouldn't be airtight. The air was stale and musty, making it difficult and unpleasant to breathe, so the air couldn't be too good, she thought.

D'oro wondered what the room might have been built for. From what she had heard about the man, she speculated again about the possibility that Clay Nalton might have used the room for a hideout. Could he have faked his death and hidden there while her father was charged with his murder? Would she be another victim of the scheme that had blighted her father's whole life?

Of all her terrified thoughts, the one that filled her with the greatest despair was the thought that she might never see Bret again. Her whole body ached for the comfort of being held close in the protection of his arms.

Chapter Twelve

Bret emerged from the mine shaft, feeling better. His raw nerves had been soothed by the therapy of hard physical labor. He squinted as the slanting rays of the setting sun hit his eyes. Thor came over to greet him more sedately than usual. He accepted a pat on the head without his accustomed exuberant welcome.

"Still blame me for the fiasco last night?" Bret asked the dog ruefully. "I guess I was a little rough on her, but she shouldn't have led me on, playing me for a fool like that."

Thor turned and walked away as if he were too polite to tell his master what he thought. When Bret started to the hoist house to put his gear away, the dog did not follow as usual, but went back to watching the bandanna on the cable.

As Bret came around the side of the hoist house the telephone was ringing insistently. He did not hurry his steps. He was in no mood to listen to Candy's petulant chatter.

"Heartbreaker Mine," he answered brusquely, hoping his words and tone would encourage the caller to think he was busy and keep it brief.

"Mr. Bret Johnson?" asked a strange feminine voice.

"Yes."

"This is Linda Blake, Doctor Drummond's nurse. The Doctor asked me to call you and tell you that Miss Annie Baxter was brought in to the hospital this afternoon with a possible concussion and other injuries. One of her horses threw her. His diagnosis wasn't complete, but Miss Baxter was asking for you. I've been trying to locate you for a couple of hours."

"Thanks. I'll be right there."

Bret loped to the trailer and bounded inside, taking the steps two at a time. He reappeared short minutes later, his hair gleaming with moisture from a shower. He was still buttoning his clean shirt as he slid into the pickup. He looked around for Thor and was puzzled but relieved to see him still watching the portal of the mine. The dog had been acting strangely all day, but he supposed he'd feel that way if he had almost attacked a friend. D'oro did have a way with his dog, he thought morosely. Anyway, it saved precious minutes not to have to give Thor the commands to stay while he went to see Annie.

Bret broke all records getting to Mariposa's small modern hospital.

"May I see Miss Annie Baxter, please?" he asked the efficient-looking receptionist, hoping that he would not be asked to explain who he was and his relationship to the patient.

The woman looked up briefly from the busy switchboard and nodded in the direction of the hallway. "Room eight."

Bret walked down the hall, conscious of the ring of his heels on the polished tile floor. He paused in the doorway, surprised to see Annie propped up in bed. Her dark hair fanned out on the pillow, framing her face. The small wing of white hair cutting through the dark served to accent the rich deep outdoor tan of her flawless complexion. The tightly drawn sheet emphasized the slender contours of her body. She certainly was an attractive woman, he thought.

She looked up then and saw him. "Bret, how nice of you to come see me. But how did you know I was here?"

Bret hesitated to say that the nurse told him she had been asking for him. "You know about the local grapevine. I heard about your accident and came right over."

"Fool horse. Fool doctor. Both too young to know what they're doing," she grumbled in her rich throaty voice, assuming the manner of old-time residents. "Old Doc Smith would have known I've been thrown too many times and my head is too hard to be seriously damaged just because a fall knocked me out. He had poor Rattlesnake scared half to death."

"And that foot? I suppose that's the doctor's imagination, too," Bret teased, greatly relieved to find her injury less serious than originally feared.

Annie scowled at her left foot, resting on a pillow to support the massive bandages. "Just a bad sprain. Twisted it under me when I landed. Doctor says I'll have to keep off it for a couple of weeks."

The staccato sound of high-heeled boots interrupted them as Rattlesnake entered, carrying a bouquet of flowers that was almost larger than he was. He set the vase on a stand in the corner and looked quickly around the room. "Where's D'oro?"

"How should I know?" snapped Bret.

"When I talked to her at the mine a couple of hours ago, she said she'd go find you," Rattlesnake answered with a belligerence that indicated D'oro was a cause for which he would take on the second major fight of his life.

"D'oro was at the Heartbreaker today?" Bret asked, again goaded by suspicion at the unusual information.

"That's what I said."

"I didn't see her car, or any tracks where she might have forded the stream."

"'Course not. She was ridin' Bonanza."

"D'oro was going to ride over to see the Silver Queen before she left today. She must have stopped by the Heartbreaker," cut in Annie as the two men glared at each other.

After last night, had she still come to say goodbye? Bret wondered. Had she been waiting for him when Rattlesnake phoned? Would she have gone down into the mine to let him know if Rattlesnake had thought it was urgent? He had known that D'oro had a special feeling for Annie the night they came back from Yosemite and she had been reluctant to have him spend the night with her at Annie's house. D'oro would have known that he was working in the tunnel, because Thor was in position by the bandanna. When Bret left, Thor had still been there by the cable. Could it be because D'oro was down in the mine?

"Tell me exactly what you told D'oro, and what her answer was," Bret said in a low urgent tone, the authority of which was not to be disputed.

"I just told her Annie had been thrown off her horse. When I called, the doctor thought maybe she'd been hurt worse 'n she was." Rattlesnake hesitated, but prompted by the probing of Bret's steely blue eyes, he continued. "I told her Annie'd been askin' for you."

Annie recalled with embarrassment that she had been trying to find Bret to talk to him about D'oro and her work before the younger woman left Mariposa. She silently acknowledged that it could have been her preoccupation with how she would handle the whole subject with Bret that had distracted her while she was mounting her horse. With a young nervous horse it took only a moment's carelessness to be thrown.

"What did D'oro say?" Bret asked Rattlesnake urgently.

"She said that you was there at the mine and that she'd tell you."

"But I never saw her." How could she have failed to find him if she'd gone down in the mine? He was working in a new straight-line tunnel with no crosscuts.

"Has D'oro ever been down in the mine?" Annie asked, quickly following Bret's line of thinking.

"I took her down last week," answered Bret with growing concern.

That information surprised Annie. She knew

how most miners felt about visitors, particularly women in a mine, but she didn't comment.

"Could she of got lost down there?" asked Rattlesnake, sensing the growing alarm of the other two.

"Not in the new tunnel where I'm working. It runs in a direct line. If she stopped at the wrong level and followed one of the old tunnels..." He shook his head and shrugged expressively.

There was a cold stark silence as each of the three considered the frightening possibilities and each blamed himself for whatever might have happened.

"Is there anyone who would know those old tunnels, who might have a working drawing?" Bret asked Annie as he began to translate his fear into a plan of action.

"Jim Gregg, D'oro's father, knew the mine well. He'd know whether there were working drawings."

"You mean your partner in the Silver Queen?" asked Bret with bitterness.

"Jim hasn't owned an interest in the Silver Queen in more than twenty years. He deeded his share to me when he left Mariposa." Annie was suddenly angrily defensive. She wondered how Bret knew Jim had been her partner. It had not come up during the deal for the Heartbreaker.

"Then how did he give it to D'oro? The clerk in the recorder's office told me half of the Silver Queen had recently been recorded in her name. He knew the property adjoined the Heartbreaker."

"I gave it to her. I had my lawyer draw up the

deed a couple of weeks ago. I just returned her rightful heritage.'' The quiet controlled anger in Annie's voice made it clear that a sprained ankle was the only thing not functioning with its usual force.

Bret felt as if someone had hit him in the stomach, knocking the wind out of him. ''Can you get hold of Gregg?''

Annie hesitated, then bit her lip. ''I'll try.''

''Hurry.'' Bret matched his actions to his words and left the hospital as fast as his long legs would carry him without breaking into a run.

With a trembling hand Annie reached for the phone on her bedside table. ''Long distance, please,'' she told the hospital switchboard operator. ''I'd like to place a call to the Plata Nueva Mine in Zacatecas, Mexico.'' The repetitions in two languages and the clicking and crackling seemed endless before a soft musical voice answered, ''Plata Nueva.''

''La oficina de Señor Griegos, por favor.'' Annie slowly said the words she thought she would never have the courage to say unless he made the first move.

''Griegos aquí,'' answered the voice, which brought all of her aching longing for him to the surface.

''Jim, it's Ann.'' She struggled desperately to keep her hunger for him out of her voice, but didn't quite succeed.

''Ann, is anything wrong?'' The concern in his voice showed all too clearly that he had not expected her to call him without reason.

"It's D'oro. We think she may be lost in the Heartbreaker Mine."

"What the hell would she be doing down there?"

"It's a long story. I haven't time to tell you now. Do you know if there were any working drawings of the mine?" She could not allow any other thoughts than her fear for D'oro's safety.

"Yes. We kept complete drawings of both mines in the office of the Silver Queen. Whoever cleaned it out might know what was done with them."

"We shouldn't have any trouble finding them, then. Everything is just the way you left it." The silence that followed the information was so long that Annie thought the connection had been broken. "I'll send Rattlesnake after them immediately," she continued when the sound of movement told her there was still someone on the other end of the line.

"Tell him they're in the file cabinet. Is there someone there who can direct the search for D'oro?" he asked, his voice that of a man used to assuming authority.

"The owner of the Heartbreaker—the man D'oro has been working for. He's a very competent mining engineer. He's the one who asked about working drawings."

"Sounds like he knows what he's doing. Tell him to call me here any hour of the day or night if there's any additional information he needs. The switchboard operator will know where to locate me." He gave her the number, which she wrote with trembling fingers, wondering if she would have the courage to call it if the need were her own.

As if her thoughts communicated themselves to him over the miles, he asked, "And you, Ann, how are you?"

"Same as always, nursing a sprained ankle from a fall off a horse," she answered lightly, not daring to hint at the pain that had been in her heart from the moment she had heard his voice.

His laugh was rich and resonant. He sounded as close as the next room, but her aching longing told her he was as far away as the moon.

"Call me when there's any news of D'oro. Take care of that ankle." There was a pause, then an almost whispered "I love you."

"Te quero," she answered, wondering how much Spanish the hovering Rattlesnake understood. The grin on his face told her she might as well have said it in English. Reluctantly she replaced the phone. She had neither the time nor the inclination to indulge in self-pity. She took a deep breath and ran her fingers through her hair, smoothing it in place. Her fingertips lingered at her temple, touching the streak of white, which had caused the Mexican gardener to identify her as El Blanco's woman. A smile flitted briefly across her face, followed by a look of determination and brusque directions to Rattlesnake. "The drawings are in the file cabinet under Heartbreaker. You know where the key is to the office of the Silver Queen."

He nodded, his voice too tight to speak. What a

woman, he thought with admiration. Though he had no suspicion of her recent detour to Mexico, he had known Annie all her life. He understood the pain that telephone call had cost her. He was glad of the errand, which sent him scurrying from her room.

The drive from the hospital to the mine took Rattlesnake a few minutes longer than it had taken Bret. The cowboy's pickup was older and not as well maintained as the young engineer's.

Bret did not park beside his trailer as usual, but drove directly to the hoist house. Thor, who had remained beside the entrance to the shaft, came trotting over to greet him.

"Is she still down there, old boy?" Bret asked as he gave the dog's head a quick pat before they each went about their business. Thor went back to watching the cable, and Bret went into the hoist house to look for any information that might have escaped his notice with the urgency of the nurse's call. He grabbed up his hard hat and the split cowhide jacket that he wore down in the mine. The other hard hat and his old wool shirt were gone, mute evidence that D'oro had indeed gone down in the mine.

The key to the laboratory was on its hook, yet there might be some clue there as to what she had been doing at the Heartbreaker that morning. Bret snatched up the key and trotted around the building to the laboratory side. When he impatiently flung open the door, the answer was there to meet him in the form of a single flask sitting on the otherwise cleared workbench. He snatched up the flask and held it up to the light. She had done it! There were glistening particles of silver-and-gold-covered lumps that he knew to be zinc pellets.

Bret grabbed up her report, which he had read before going down in the mine that morning; the report he had left lying beside the typewriter. He flipped through the familiar pages to the note at the end. Arsenic! The inhibitor had been arsenic, which threw the entire process off. He had been stupid not to realize the importance of the arsenic, which he knew to be in the ore, but he had been stupid about far more important things, he thought bitterly. He recalled how he had laughed when he heard her fling the word chauvinist after him when she thought he was out of earshot. But she had been right about that, too. He just couldn't accept the lovely creature as a serious scientist or as the woman his heart told him she was. He thumped down the report and strode out the door, slamming and locking it behind him. He did not take the time to return the key to the hoist house, but thrust it in his pocket. Bret sprinted to the mine shaft and was down the ladder with the speed of a fireman after the alarm has sounded. He jogged the familiar length of the drift where he was working, not really expecting to find anything there, then he returned to the level above where he was working. It would be very easy for anyone not familiar with the mine to stop a level too soon.

Bret had cleared and worked that level extensively before going down to start the new drift. He knew it to be a rabbit warren of intersecting tunnels. Apparently, rich pockets of ore had been found in several places along its length, and as each gave out, attempts to locate the main vein had been made on both sides. Methodically working a grid pattern, he searched each intersecting tunnel as he went. When he finally reached the end, he noticed that his light was dimming perceptibly. He looked at his watch. It was not yet nine o'clock. He would need more batteries for the long night ahead.

His climb up the ladder was slowed not by the heaviness in his legs but by the heaviness in his heart. He was reluctant to leave the search for D'oro for even that short interruption. When he emerged from the shaft, Thor greeted him as expected, followed by Rattlesnake. The small man triumphantly held aloft a roll of drawings.

"Right where Jim said they were," he announced.

Bret did not take the time to pursue the implications of that information, but accepted the drawings gratefully. He hesitated a moment, then took them into the laboratory and spread the drawings on the workbench—*D'oro's* workbench, he thought with desperation.

"Anythin' I can do to help?"

"I need more batteries for my searchlight."

"We've got some at the ranch. I'll get them 'n' be back in 'bout twenty minutes. I'll bring the horse trailer and take Bonanza home."

"Where did you find him?"

"Tied in a clearin' back behind your trailer."

The faint hope Bret had been clinging to that

D'oro was not down in the mine vanished. He had kept telling himself without really believing it that she might have ridden off somewhere else after she talked to Rattlesnake; that he had been misinterpreting Thor's actions.

The working drawings of the Heartbreaker Mine were detailed and accurate in the areas where Bret was familiar with the mine. They were obviously professionally done, and Bret noted with chagrin that the initials at the end were J.G. Somehow the tragedy of the Silver Queen, which Bret had taken pains to ferret out, had projected itself into the very core of his life, creating the gnawing anxiety he faced.

As he focused his attention on the drawings spread on the workbench, the room was so filled with D'oro's presence, he could almost hear her voice saying words he hadn't really listened to before. He examined the drawings so minutely, he could practically reproduce them from memory by the time Rattlesnake returned with the batteries and the sandwiches and coffee Lupe had prepared. Bret choked down the food, tasteless as it was to him, because he knew the demands of that night would require all of his strength. He declined Rattlesnake's offer to work down in the tunnel with him, knowing what courage the offer cost the small cowboy. Bret had often heard him say "Wouldn't catch me down in one of them mines for a million dollars."

Chapter Thirteen

Annie Baxter, successful businesswoman and community leader, swung into action. It was no time to sit around and daydream like a schoolgirl, she told herself sternly. She started Lupe making sandwiches and filling thermoses with coffee to sustain whoever might need it through the long night ahead. Annie had asked Lupe's husband, Manuel, to pick her up, and over the protests of the doctor, she was out of the hospital in twenty minutes. She moved slowly with the aid of crutches, a reluctant compromise when the doctor insisted she must keep her weight off the injured ankle for a couple of weeks. Annie was waiting at the hospital entrance when Manuel arrived.

In spite of all of her efforts, an irate Annie reached the ranch minutes after Rattlesnake departed with batteries and some of Lupe's sandwiches and coffee in the horse van. It galled her not to go directly to the scene of the action, but she knew there was nothing she could do there, and awkward as she was hobbling around, she might be in the way.

The time of waiting seemed interminable until Annie saw the familiar lights of the horse trailer out through the darkness at the bend of the road by the cottonwood grove. She heard Rattlesnake drive into the corral and unload Bonanza before coming to report.

"The mine drawins' was right where Jim said they was. Bret said they ought to do it, unless there had been additional work besides Gregg's on the mine. Took him extra batteries for his light and the sandwiches and coffee Lupe fixed for him. Told him I'd be back after I got Bonanza home, but he said weren't nothin' nobody could help him with till daylight. D'oro must 'a took the extra hard hat. But Bret don't want anyone else down there trompin' around over her tracks if she left any 'fore he has a go at it."

"In that case, don't let anyone know she's missing until I tell you to. Warn Lupe and Manuel. I'll tell the woman on the hospital switchboard to tell any callers that I'm sleeping. My friends are pretty used to my getting a little banged up around the horses. They'll have heard I'm in the hospital, so we can keep this line free if Bret has any news or needs anything. Hope you haven't told anyone."

"Haven't had time to," he said, masking his eagerness to be doing something with feigned complaint.

"Well, come along. We'll eat some of those sandwiches Lupe's been keeping herself busy making." The old friends faced each other across the kitchen table and each forced himself to choke down a couple of the sandwiches in order to encourage the other one to do so. The pungent coffee helped wash them down. Neither attempted conversation.

When Rattlesnake left for the bunkhouse, Annie finally convinced Lupe she could manage perfectly well alone and sent the housekeeper home. She tried to focus attention on a television program, but they had never seemed so banal and stupid. Never had the house seemed so empty as it did when she hobbled awkwardly to her room. The crutches echoing hollowly on the tile seemed to mock the hollowness of her future. Annie had just started to undress when she heard Rattlesnake's pickup leaving. She understood all too well his restlessness and wondered what errand he had invented to occupy himself. She knew there had been no call from Bret. The phone rang in the main house and had to be transferred to the bunkhouse extension.

Balanced on one foot and one crutch, even simple routine tasks were awkward and time consuming. Finally she dropped her lacy apricot silk nightgown over her head and stood surveying herself in the mirror. It was a mighty fancy getup for a ranch woman her age, she mocked herself. The gown was part of the collection of feminine lingerie that she told herself was her secret vice. She climbed awkwardly into the big bed and allowed herself to revel in the bittersweet memory of Jim's voice. Had she made a mistake not urging him to come? Her own longing to see him so clouded her judgment, she wasn't sure. There didn't seem to be anything Jim could do that Bret wasn't already doing.

When she heard Rattlesnake's pickup return, Annie knew he couldn't stay still, yet he wouldn't let himself be long away from the place where the first news would be received if—when—Bret found something. She wondered if he had driven to the mine.

Her thoughts were interrupted by a light, tentative knock on the front door. Annie sprang out of bed, sending shock waves of pain through her sprained ankle. Uttering an oath that would have done justice to a horse trainer, she grabbed one crutch and balanced against it while she maneuvered into her robe and cinched the belt around her waist. She grabbed the other crutch and thumped her way through the house with a speed suitable for the Founder's Day three-legged race. Breathlessly she jerked open the door to confront an apparition. The full moon gleamed eerily off a thatch of snow-white hair framing the face that had not been out of her thoughts since she had heard his voice hours before.

"Jim, you came!"

"Didn't you know I would?"

For how many years had she dreamed of the day he would walk through that door? She suddenly realized that being with him in Mexico was not the same as having him here, whatever the reason. She smiled and held out her arms to him. He took away her crutches and carried her to the big leather chair in the family room, then settled comfortably in the chair, cuddling her on his lap and kissing her as if he had just returned home from a long journey.

"How in the world?" she spluttered when she could catch her breath.

"When I talked to you, I didn't know whether the company plane was available. It was the only way I could get here in time to do any good. I called our pilot, and he said he could be ready to take off in thirty minutes. When I called Mariposa airport for clearance to land, Rattlesnake heard me on his CB radio. Somehow he recognized the name Griegos."

"He was at the hospital when I called you," she said, recalling the concerned way Rattlesnake had listened to her end of the conversation.

"He was at the airport waiting by the time we were on the ground. I had planned to go directly to the mine, but he said there was nothing I could do until daylight. He wasn't sure that even if he was with me the miner's big watchdog would let me near the place in the dark, so I decided to stay here till daylight. My pilot is bunking with Rattlesnake. I didn't want to disturb you, so I was just going to sleep there, too. Rattlesnake said the only thing in the world he was afraid of was you when you were mad, and you would sure be mad if I didn't come to the house." He chuckled with the deep warm sound that sent ripples of pleasure through her. He kissed her again, but with an air of distraction that told her there were questions on his mind that he was impatient to ask. Just having him there was enough. She rested her head on his chest and waited.

"Now, about that long story. What would D'oro be doing down in the Heartbreaker Mine?"

"It's all my fault. I seem to wreck everything I touch that is dear to you."

"That's a pretty harsh judgment because a healthy young woman spends a night lost in a gold mine. You were the one reminding me she's all grown up. Suppose you start at the beginning."

Annie was not deceived by his words. His being there was a far graver assessment of the situation. "Well, the repeat experiment was a failure, just as it was for Juan. I think D'oro and Bret must have had a fight over it. She was ready to leave today, but I had to meddle." Self-accusation was bitter in her voice, but that time he did not interrupt. "I asked her to wait until I got back from an appointment. I went to talk to Bret at the rail siding where he is loading a shipment of ore for the smelter, but he wasn't there."

"He must have decided several days ago that the formula wasn't going to work."

"I guess none of us showed much faith in her work. I think that may have been part of the problem. I knew she was going to ride over to the Silver Queen before she left." She felt every fiber in his body stiffen at the mention of the ill-fated mine. She did not look at him, but hurried on with her account. "I didn't want to pass her on the road to the mines, so I took the two-year-old out for a workout. He was a little stiff from riding in the van. My mind must have been more on what I wanted to say to Bret than on what I was doing and I let the fool horse throw me. I hit my head on something and had a slight concussion. Rattlesnake fussed over me like an old hen. Rushed me off to the hospital. He heard me mumbling about Bret and thought I had some kind of a dying wish to see him or something." She could feel his eyes searching her face.

Annie met his look with an honesty in her clear brown eyes that brought gentleness back into the arms holding her. "He was wrong on both counts, of course. I must have been sort of rehearsing the things I wanted to say to Bret when I fell, and the ideas kept on spinning like a broken record. Well, like an angel of gloom and doom Rattlesnake called the mine. D'oro answered the phone. For some reason she'd gone back to the laboratory. She must have believed Rattlesnake's fantasy and gone off to notify Bret, who was working in the tunnel. The whole thing would be damn funny if something hadn't gone wrong. Like you said, here I am the most self-sufficient woman in these parts and everyone going in circles trying to look after me."

He laughed then in spite of his concern and lightly kissed the tip of her nose. "Have you found a producer for this soap opera?" he asked lightly, and saw the deep look of anguish in her eyes give way to a tentative smile.

Closing the subject, he said matter-of-factly, "Rattlesnake said he found the plans without any trouble, and that this Bret was using them as a grid in his search. He wants to look at the entry to each level for footprints before anyone else joins him in the search. I'd have to agree with his methods.''

As he had in all the years she had known him, Jim had managed to lift the burden from her shoulders onto his own so that she could turn to the soft things of being a woman. She invited him to the kitchen and fed him some of Lupe's sandwiches, often forgetting the pretense of eating one herself as her eyes feasted on the nearness of him.

Finally he carried her to the big hand-carved bed, a model for the one where they had made passionate love. Could it have been just a short time ago? It seemed like another lifetime.

She felt him hesitate as he entered the master bedroom. The specter of Clay Nalton had blighted the promise of happiness they had found in Mexico, and he haunted that room as well. If only Jim had taken her to the guest room as he had on that night so long ago when she had needed him so desperately. But D'oro's presence was there. Would her home forever be possessed by ghosts? With sudden decision she resolved there was one ghost who would be laid to rest that night.

Jim placed her gently in the shallow valley in the middle of the big bed, its shape giving mute testimony to the many years she had slept there alone. His action confirmed her premonition. She looked into his clear gray eyes and found a deep and haunted sorrow in them and could sense the direction his thoughts were taking him. Before he could kiss her cheek and mumble excuses about her needing rest, she gently wrapped her arms around his neck, tangling her fingers in the thick springy hair at the back of his head. With the strength and quickness of an expert horsewoman she rolled away from him, surprising him and catching him off-balance. Though he braced his hands on each side of her to support part of his weight, he came thudding down on top of her. His surprised laugh was low and intimate and so close to her ear, she could feel the warmth of his breath. She knew she was winning. Ghosts couldn't stand to be laughed at. However, she knew the one she was battling was both persistent and cunning. She lowered her mouth to the pulse in his throat, caressing it with her lips, teasing it with her tongue until she could feel the rapid drumbeat of his heart. His mouth answered the invitation of hers, kissing and being kissed with complete abandon. Her hands moved from his neck across his broad shoulders to the lean hardness of his waist, still as flat and tight as the day she had first seen him. One of her hands found its way under his shirt, and she trailed her fingers lightly up the hollow of his backbone. He shivered with delight, then his lips burned searing kisses from her mouth to the lobe of her ear and he whispered huskily, "You are a wanton woman." The words sounded strangely like a caress.

The wisp of apricot silk she had been wearing went with him when he left her bed ever so briefly to finish removing his shirt and slacks. There wasn't the slightest doubt he'd be right back. Their final acts of lovemaking were not the carefree blazing passion of the night in Zacatecas.

They were marked by the deep solace and contentment that only those who have had a long and caring relationship can find in times of trouble in each other's arms, each other's bodies.

The first faint streaks of dawn tinged the sky when he left her. Through lowered lashes she watched him dress quickly and move stealthily from the room. She did not allow any slight movement, any change in her rate of breathing to betray the fact that she was awake, as here was another need for his strength.

Chapter Fourteen

Bret stood on the familiar platform of his working level, more weary and discouraged than he could recall having been in his life before. After Rattlesnake left and he had started back down the shaft, he forced himself to stop at each landing. There was no thought in his mind that D'oro might have mistakenly followed one of the upper drifts. She was too smart for that. However, something other than being lost might have caused her to turn off any of the platforms. He tried not to think of the possibility of a fall, but every contingency had to be faced. Below the level where groundwater seeped to glisten on the wet face of the shaft, he began to search every tunnel that was not blocked by debris and to mentally check them off against the working drawings. He had checked carefully for any evidence of a new rockslide that might have prevented her from returning to the surface.

Brooding fear assailed him when he finally reached the levels he had already checked. Only one last chance remained, what he jokingly called his basement. The shaft continued one more level below the new drift. It was there that he had installed the pulley and gears for his hoist. There the tunnel leading off the shaft had no crosscuts and gave little evidence of having been worked much. It was more likely a service area for the old mine. The working drawings showed it as short and without any special interest. To reach it, D'oro would have had to bypass his working level, which hardly seemed likely. The floor of the basement was solid rock. Surely she would have known that they stopped on a wooden platform.

Then he remembered that she might not have known. He recalled that she had tripped on his sneak-thief step and that he had lifted her off the ladder into his arms. With an empty ache he could imagine her there now. He remembered how she had slipped her arms around his neck, inviting his kiss. With some stupid resolve about not mixing business and pleasure, he had resisted his desire for her. What a pompous fool he had been.

Convinced that D'oro could be, had to be, somewhere in that lower level, Bret scuttled down the final section of ladder. He carefully examined the landing, but the rock was too solid to show footprints if there had been any. He moved quickly along the tunnel without finding any impediment. In his anxiety it seemed that the tunnel was longer than indicated on the drawings. Yes, he was sure of it. The tunnel was longer. Odd, it was the only inaccuracy he had found in the carefully prepared plans. Finally his lamp reflected back to him from a solid wall of quartz. He had arrived at the end of the tunnel, and she was not there. He had searched every foot of the mine, but D'oro had simply vanished, even though everything pointed to her still being down there somewhere. Bret put his hands on the solid wall in front of him and leaned wearily on it. In a few hours, at daybreak, they would organize a search party. There wasn't a miner in the area who wouldn't volunteer when a friend of Annie's was involved, but he didn't know what a bunch of men, even professionals, tromping around could do that he hadn't done.

Painfully Bret recalled the day he had brought D'oro down in the mine. If he hadn't done so, she might never have tried to go down alone. He hadn't really thought that going down would help with her failure in the laboratory. It was an impulse when he watched her through the laboratory window, almost in tears, yet with her stubborn jaw set, going grimly back to work on the process. She said she wanted to see the workings of the mine, and he thought it would take her mind off her problem for a few hours. It seemed to work. There were those wonderful moments when she sat beside him in the dark in perfect harmony with him and his world. He was so sure it was his world. The Heartbreaker Mine offered such challenge, he had put everything he owned into it, even his car. He thought he had won. The strike had been rich. Even after shipping and smelter charges the operation was profitable beyond his expectations. He should have let it go at that instead of trying to build his find into a community project as Baxter had done. D'oro's work sitting on the bench in the laboratory gave him the means to make even that dream come true, but without her to share it, the mine would still live up to its name: heartbreaker.

Systematically reviewing every detail of the drawing of the mine in his mind, Bret slumped down on the hard rock floor and stretched his tired legs in front of him. He turned off his lamp and laid his hat beside him, so he could lean his cramped shoulders against the end wall of the tunnel. He could almost feel D'oro's gentle, vibrant presence beside him. His hand reached out as it had before, but found only rough cold rock. Then his fingers caught on a cut surface his tired eyes had not seen. He snatched up his light and stared in bewilderment at a symmetrically cut rock the size of a man's shoulders. The bottom of the hewed-out rock was recessed almost an inch behind the surrounding wall. He crashed his foot against the cut rock so hard, he almost fell through the opening when it gave way. Incredibly the rock did not slide backward or drop out of position, it swung upward from the bottom as if it were on a hinge! He grabbed up the trenching shovel he had been carrying in case he should find her trapped by a rockslide. He wedged the short sturdy shovel to support the bottom of the stone in its raised position. There could be no doubt that it was some kind of a trapdoor held in position by a stout spring.

Kneeling, he shone the beam of the powerful flashlight he had been using into the opening behind the rock. He was looking into a small room cut or blasted out of the rock a few feet below the floor of the tunnel where he was. The carved-out rock cave had not been shown on the working drawings of the mine. He was sure of that. Shining the light around the walls, he saw a pile of mildewed army blankets stacked against the far wall with an old canteen and some small cardboard boxes beside them. Behind the blankets a pile of loose rock looked as if it might cover the entrance to another tunnel leading from the far side of the cave. He brought the beam of light back across the floor of the cave toward himself. There lay D'oro at the base of the ledge on which he was perched. She was so pale and still, she looked as if she were dead!

Bret dropped through the opening in the rock as rapidly as if he was evading a blow from an enemy. Frantically he placed his fingers to the hollow of her throat, searching for a pulse. She felt so cold, so terribly cold! He resisted the almost overpowering urge to grab her up and crush her to the warmth of his body. He jerked off his jacket and covered her with it. Gently he raised her chin and tilted her head backward. He pried open her jaw, gritted against the cold, and covered her mouth with his, breathing his warmth and his strength into her cold stiff body.

D'oro's fragile floating dream of searching endlessly for Bret through a frozen land of ice-crystal trees and glistening snowdrifts began to fade. She could feel his lips covering hers with all the gentleness and caring she had longed to find in him.

His mouth asked nothing of her, made no demands—it only gave. She could feel the warmth of his breath across her thick parched tongue, down her dry aching throat. Her whole being was in complete accord with his. Their very breathing seemed to be in perfect unison.

His warm clever fingers found the pulse at her throat, then glided over her breasts to the cleavage between them. His hand caressed, coaxed until the beating of her heart raced to meet his hand. His fingers moved across the ivory-smooth skin of her shoulders and down her arm, bringing a pulsing warmth like hot tea poured into a glass of ice. It was only when he removed his other hand that she realized he had been holding her nose while he breathed life back into her oxygen-starved body. She was familiar with the ancient custom of some of Mexico's indians that when a person saves another's life, he becomes responsible for that life. In her half-conscious state she felt she truly belonged to Bret.

He took off her boots and socks, stroking her slender well-arched feet as if they were pieces of priceless sculpture. He teased her toes as one might a baby's until they were suffused with glowing warmth, then he nuzzled her foot against his cheek, shadowed by the long hours of his search.

Sliding one hand under her knees and the other under her shoulders, he lifted her tenderly in his arms and held her close against the warmth of his body. Slowly the heavy, dragging weight she felt in her arms responded to the orders from her heart and they crept around his neck as if to make sure of her hold on life. She lifted leaden eyelids in response to his close scrutiny of her face.

"The most beautiful eyes in the world, the color of molten silver," he murmured, brushing her eyelids lightly with his lips.

"Bret, you found me," she murmured through numbed lips.

"The most precious treasure I ever prospected for, and the hardest to find." He looked around him at the small hollowed-out grotto it had taken a miracle for him to find. Focusing his attention upward to the ledge on which he had been resting, he could see the back of the rock that covered the entry and the spring that held it in place. Wedged into the spring behind the door was a flattened miners' tin hat. That was what had moved the door far enough out of position for him to see that it was separate from the rest of the rock surrounding it. Astonished, he looked around the room for the tool she had used to flatten the hat and wedge it in place. Near where she had been lying was a small battered can marked "Chopped Ham." He gently removed her right arm from around his neck and unwound the tattered strip of army blanket wrapped around her hand. He looked at the palm covered with bruises and dried blood and tenderly raised it to his lips like a parent kissing away the hurt of a child.

D'oro's eyelids flickered briefly again and she softly whispered, "So tired," as she nestled her head in the hollow of his shoulder.

What a courageous scrapper she was! She was the woman he knew would help him build his dreams. Could it have been only yesterday that he had set the stage so carefully to ask her to marry him? At the last minute there had been the trip to the recorder's office for his ownership certificate. Like a fool he had listened to the clerk's idle gossip about D'oro being a new partner in the Silver Queen and had jumped to vicious, stupid conclusions. If he had just had faith in her, they both might have been spared so much! He hoped that when she was fully conscious and her memory returned, she would be half as forgiving as she was right now.

As he moved toward the opening his foot brushed the small can she had used for a hammer, and it rolled against the box of C rations from which it had been taken. Watching it, he saw the still legible date on the box, 1960. My God! The secrets of the room hadn't been found in more than twenty years. Except for the courage and grim determination of the woman resting so lightly in his arms, he might not have found it in time. The thought made a cold shudder run through him. His arms tightened possessively around her.

Bret heard a sound above him and looked up. If he had been a superstitious man, he would have been certain he was seeing a ghost. The eyes looking back at him seemed to be only reflections of his light with no other color. Wisps of white hair showed beneath a miners' hat so long out of use, he had seen the type only in souvenir stores. The broad shoulders that followed the head through the hole were covered with a coarse hand-loomed wool jacket fastened with buttons of tooled Mexican silver.

"Is she alive?" the specter asked in halting tones.

"Yes. She was unconscious from lack of oxygen, but with the door opened artificial respiration revived her. She's just tired and cold and showing some symptoms of light shock."

The man Bret knew to be her father reached out his arms for D'oro. Reluctantly Bret handed her up to him, forcing himself to admit that it was certainly quicker than having to maneuver the two of them up over that ledge alone.

Unhampered, Bret was up the ledge and standing beside them almost before Jim could get to his feet with his daughter in his arms.

"Let me take her now. There's something back down there I think you should see. I'm Bret Johnson. You're Gregg?"

Jim seemed startled at hearing the name he hadn't used in twenty years. He responded as reluctantly as Bret had to the demands of the outstretched arms for his precious burden, though his mind told him the young miner who had found her had every right. He kissed his daughter's cheek and saw her eyelids flutter, then he placed her in the other man's arms. He watched the broad back of the man whose height almost matched his own forcing him to stoop forward to avoid the uneven top of the tunnel.

Jim dropped agilely from the ledge on which he was standing into the cave where Bret and D'oro had been. Running Rattlesnake's flashlight around the walls, he was as stunned as if he had been hit. He examined the pile of mildewed blanets and the boxes of C rations on which he read the date with dawning comprehension. The hideout had been there at the time he was working the Silver Queen, yet he had not known of its existence. He pried at the pile of loose rocks and confirmed that there was a tunnel behind them, a tunnel that could only connect with one from the Silver Queen. It confirmed his suspicions that Clay Nalton had been high-grading the ore, hand selecting and stealing the pieces that held chunks of almost pure silver. Having dug a connecting tunnel from the Silver Queen to the Heartbreaker, which they weren't operating at the time, he had the perfect way to remove large quantities of the most valuable ore. He didn't begrudge Clay the silver, only the years of which he had robbed him. He knew that after Clay signaled him to start the hoist, he would have had time to duck into a concealed opening Jim hadn't known was there while Jim moved back from the top of the shaft to the hoist controls. He wondered if the faked accident had been part of Clay's plan from the start to cover his disappearance, or if he had seized on it after Jim warned him to stay away from Ann. The whole thing was so typical of Clay, yet as he had stood looking at the horror of the accident the thought had never occurred to him.

Looking more closely at the floor, Jim could see the deep scrape marks where ore buckets had been dragged. He turned his light around the walls of the small room, stopping to examine the trapdoor. When he saw the flattened metal hat that

D'oro had managed to force beneath the spring, moving the door enough for Bret to find it, he snatched the hat from his own head.

"Oh, my God!" They were the same, a style of miners' hat that had been worn twenty years earlier. It was a different shape from the one Bret had been wearing and the one lying at the base of the wall, which apparently D'oro had worn. Jim remembered the day the salesman had gone to the Silver Queen and he and Clay had each bought one of the new style of hats. He carefully examined the hat he was holding, which he had found in Rattlesnake's pickup. There could be no doubt it was his own. Rattlesnake must have picked it up when he went to the Silver Queen for the drawings. The one holding the spring had to be Clay's. It was the hat Clay had waved to signal him to start the hoist the day he was believed to have been killed. D'oro had found it in this room! There could be no doubt Clay had ducked into a secret opening to the tunnel when Jim had moved back from the top of the shaft to the hoist controls.

Jim could feel the evil that surrounded him with a clamminess like the dead hand of the past laid on his shoulder. A shudder ran through him as he climbed from the hole where so many of his dreams had been buried. As he made his way grimly down the tunnel he thought if D'oro had been the final victim of Clay Nalton's greed and malice, he would have hunted the bastard down to the ends of the earth.

Able to move faster than Bret had, Jim caught

up with him as he reached the point where the tunnel joined the shaft.

"I think the hoist would be the fastest way to get her to the surface from my working level just above us," Bret said when he could stand erect in the shaft. "Can you operate the hoist?"

A look of pain and haunted memory flashed across the older man's face, causing Bret to recall the mess of tangled cables of the Silver Queen. Before Jim had time to reply Bret continued. "Since I'm more familiar with my hoist, it might work better the other way. You ride the bucket with her." As if the matter were settled, Bret shifted D'oro to a fireman's carry and scrambled up the short ladder to his working level.

Wordlessly Jim climbed into the ore bucket and held out his arms for his daughter. D'oro stirred briefly, then nestled into his arms, drifting back into the protective world of sleep. It seemed to Jim like the replay of an old nightmare as he stood at the bottom of a shaft with his daughter in his arms, waiting for a man on the surface to start the hoist. Though he had never seen anyone make better time on the ladders, it seemed to him he waited a lifetime holding in his arms the only good thing that had come out of the whole incredible mess.

He could hear the start of the compressor, the engaging of gears, then the bucket began to move slowly upward. As the bucket moved up past successive levels, the misty ghosts of the past were replaced by an engineer's very practical admiration of a superb piece of work by a fellow mining engineer. As precisely as a passenger elevator, the ore bucket halted level with the platform. Bret's long strides covered the distance between the hoist controls and the bucket in less time than it took Jim's eyes to adjust to the bright sunlight of the surface. As Bret took D'oro from him and he climbed out, he could see Annie leaning on a cane, with Rattlesnake hovering beside her.

"You and Jim take the Porsche. Rattlesnake and I will follow in the pickup," she directed, handing Bret her keys.

Jim had only time to brush her cheek with a kiss of gratitude for so many things before hurrying to climb into the sleek fast sports car so that Bret could put his daughter in his lap.

Bret drove the powerful car as if he were qualifying for a road race. Aware of the easy familiarity with which Bret handled Ann's car, Jim fought down the unbidden surge of male jealousy and possessiveness. He would not allow himself to question whether Ann had found a brief respite in the young miner's arms from the long years of loneliness he had imposed on her as well as himself.

The swaying of the car as it went from the mine road onto the highway caused D'oro's eyelids to flutter.

"Daddy, you did come. It wasn't a dream," she murmured against his chest like a sleepy child.

"Of course I came, baby. But I wasn't the one who found you. It was Bret who found you."

So that part wasn't a dream, either, her confused thoughts recalled. A contented smile spread slowly over her face. There were so many questions she wanted to ask those two grim-faced men who seemed to have been passing her back and forth between them in some sort of a ritual dance, but she was just too tired to keep her eyes open while the beautiful sunlight warmed her face.

Bret braked smoothly to a stop at the emergency entrance to Mariposa's hospital. He jerked open the passenger door and lifted D'oro into his arms for the finale of their strange ritual. He ignored the orderlies who had been alerted to their arrival and marched determinedly toward the room a nurse indicated. Jim stopped at the admissions desk to make the practical arrangements for his daughter. The small hospital was mercifully not one of the commercial institutions that leave patients sitting in the hall while assuring themselves that they will be paid for their services. "You can see your daughter as soon as the doctor completes his examination. We'll call you," the nurse told him when the arrangements were complete.

Annie and Rattlesnake had arrived in his battered pickup by the time the paperwork battle was completed. Jim hurried across the parking lot to lift another woman into his arms—a slightly smaller woman who had come toward him, hobbling with a cane. He kissed her with the joy and choked emotion of a man coming home from war, then he carried her to a secluded bench shaded by a tall pine tree on the hospital grounds.

"It's over," he said simply. "All the doubt, all the guilt. I'm sure Clay is alive, or was after the accident, when he had ducked into a secret passage between the Silver Queen and the Heartbreaker. That's where Bret found D'oro. She had stumbled into Clay's hideout and been trapped when the handle broke off the trapdoor. Clay was high-grading the Silver Queen.''

Annie shuddered uncontrollably. Forcing her mind back through the veil she had dropped over painful memories, she said haltingly, "I should have suspected it. He had been gone five days when he came home that last time. I thought it was another woman. It wouldn't have been the first time. He reeked of whiskey and perspiration, but there was a mustiness about him. I can almost smell it now." She shuddered again, and Jim's arm tightened around her.

Annie took a deep breath and continued. "It's so like Clay, the greed, the vicious cunning. His brothers must have known the truth. That's why they did no more than put up a good show over Clay's assumed death. How vengefully Clay must have laughed if he knew what we went through."

Jim stopped the bitter flow of her memories with his lips. He held her against him as protectively as he had watched Bret hold D'oro. "We've lost enough time on the past. I don't want to give it another precious second. As soon as we've assured ourselves that D'oro is all right, my pilot will fly us to Las—to Reno to be married. You will marry me?" he asked with a touching uncertainty.

"I thought you'd never ask." Her glib answer was too close to the truth to be as offhanded as she had intended. "What about Clay? You said he's still alive."

"He's been declared legally dead. We'll check with your lawyer, of course, but I'm sure that judgment holds good. He's been gone for twenty-six years. I'm sure he would have to appear in court in person to challenge the ruling of legally dead. By now there should be enough sheriffs, including the local one, looking for Clay that there's no danger of his resurfacing. Now, how about that wedding?"

"I would feel old and decrepit walking into the chapel on a cane. Don't you think we should wait until my ankle heels?"

"It didn't seem to bother last night. Besides, if you can't walk, I'll carry you." Seeing her hesitate, he continued with a mischievous grin. "Of course, if you want to wait, I could use a little bachelor vacation over in Vegas, say a little drinking and gambling."

People who knew Annie Baxter well wouldn't have believed how meekly she said, "We'll be married whenever you say, dear."

His laugh was husky as his kiss demonstrated his impatience all too clearly.

"Could we wait until D'oro's well enough to go with us? I'd like to have her there," she asked with more of her usual spirit.

"Thank you, sweetheart, for being so understanding. I'd like that. Now it should be about time to go see that young lady."

They found D'oro all cleaned up and sitting in a hospital bed. Her right hand was neatly bandaged and her left hand clung tightly to Bret's, her fingers entwined in his. He had apparently used the time of her examination to get washed up himself and to charm a nurse into finding him a razor.

"How's my girl?" Jim asked, dropping a kiss on his daughter's forehead.

"The doctor says I'm fine. He wants me to rest here tonight, but says I can go home in the morning."

Looking at her, Jim thought someone had already found a panacea for much of the exhaustion and inertia that had kept D'oro so still in his arms.

"If you feel up to it, we'll fly to Reno tomorrow. Ann and I are going to be married there."

"I'm so glad!" To prove her point she withdrew her hand from Bret's and held out her arms to embrace Annie. "Of course I'll feel up to it. You've waited years too long already. Will you live in Mexico?"

"No. I'd like to reopen the Silver Queen if the present owners are willing. I'd like to prove to those people who believed in me that their judgment was right, that Clay Nalton's body is not at the bottom of that shaft. It was his hideout you stumbled into."

"After tomorrow you'll be one of the owners of the Silver Queen. This is a community property state, you know," Annie said, smiling up at him. "You'll have to get D'oro's vote for the other half. I deeded it to her two weeks ago."

News of the gift did not come as a surprise to D'oro. In his halting apology Bret had mentioned

Annie's transfer of part of the mine to D'oro. She knew then was not the time to discuss long-range financial arrangements about the property within what was going to be a family. Instead her eyes sparkled with mischief as she turned them on her father. "I think I could agree to your reopening the Silver Queen if you process the ore in our mill."

"D'oro found the way to make the Rodriguez Process work. The problem was the arsenic. I expect to have the mill operating within the year," Bret cut in proudly, his large hand again covering D'oro's possessively.

Jim laughed so loud, it brought a nurse to the door with a finger to her lips. "Wait until I tell Juan." A warning look from Annie told him then was not the time to divulge Juan's personal involvement in the search for a solution. "I'll call him as soon as we get home and let him know you're all right. He'll be proud of his star pupil." It only occurred to Jim after he said it how right it was to speak of the ranch as home. He put his arm around his promised bride and urged her gently toward the door.

Out in the parking lot Annie found she had underestimated the small-town grapevine. Half of Mariposa was there, her neighbors and her friends, many of whom had been Jim's friends. Her ears caught such words as *Clay's hideout, highgrading* and *sneaky bastard*. She knew that Rattlesnake, who always seemed to be unobtrusively in the background, had overheard her conversation with Jim.

There was such a rush of handshakes and hugs, she felt like a bride already. She greeted each old-time resident by name to bridge Jim's difficulty in connecting names and faces after twenty-six years. Well liked as she was, she knew many of those people were there especially for Jim. She could sense in them the town's pride in being proved right in its judgment and its justice so many years ago.

When the opportunity presented itself, she whispered to Jim, "I think we owe these people a party."

"I think we owe them a wedding. How long would it take us to be ready?"

"Wakes and weddings are the two things a mining town does best. I think we could make it by Friday, as long as you stay here at the ranch and help." She grinned impishly.

For the first time in a long time he remembered what it was he liked about the town. He picked Annie up in a big bear hug, kissed her soundly, then shouted his invitation to their neighbors to share their newfound happiness.

Chapter Fifteen

D'oro stealthily slipped her leg out from under the sheet and raised it upward until her foot was above her head, then she let it drop with full dead weight. Bret, sleeping beside her on the water bed, bounced as if he were on a trampoline. His eyes flew open.

"What the—" A grin spread across his face. He grabbed for her and caught her as she tried to slip out of bed. He pulled her close against him, creating a veritable tidal wave. When the bed had subsided to a gentle rocking, his warm breath tickled her ear as he whispered, "Impatient this morning?"

His kiss promised that it really would be a very good morning. D'oro's body felt warm and soft and safe in his arms. He ran his fingertips lightly down her spine, causing her to shiver, then acting as if he thought she were cold, he pulled her even closer against him.

She opened her mouth to speak, but he had a better way of communicating. His lips closed over hers, and his kiss and the light strokes of his fingers on her face were tantalizingly slow, as if he had all day to make love to her and expected to spend most of it that way.

When he had kissed her until she was breathless, his lips moved down her graceful throat to the smooth flesh of her shoulder, the color of a ripe peach in the autumn sun. Halfheartedly she protested, "We have a wedding to go to."

"I thought I married you three days ago." His blue eyes crinkled at the corners in little creases that drew her fingers to them.

"Seems to me I vaguely remember something like that." D'oro laughed with a light huskiness. "It was convenient that Dad forgot to cancel his arrangements before we used them. The minister did seem a little surprised to see us show up instead of Annie and Dad, though." She giggled at the memory of the confused minister's face.

"What time is their wedding today?"

"Noon."

"Plenty of time." His stubble-covered chin tickled and teased the soft flesh of her breasts without getting close enough to scratch, only enough to make her giggle again.

Her fingers, tangled in his thick hair, denied that she was going anywhere right away, but her conscience voiced its good intentions. "I should go over early and see what I can do to help."

"You don't know much about a ranch wedding, do you? People will be falling all over each other trying to help. All you have to do is arrive, looking beautiful to complete the family picture. What are you going to wear?"

"They are beautiful together, aren't they? I found a blue chiffon dress the color of the stones in my wedding ring in one of the shops in Reno. I love the way chiffon feels on my body."

Bret's fingers glided down D'oro's enticing curves as lightly as the touch of chiffon, bringing more warmth and excitement than the most glamorous dress ever could. She snuggled close against him.

His warm breath caressed her cheek as he whispered, "You do like the ring, then?" She found his uncertainty strangely endearing. "The jeweler said you could exchange it if you didn't."

"Exchange it! I love it. It's the color of your eyes." She raised her hand from the back of his neck and extended her hand to admire again the diamond-circled sapphire the brilliant blue of his eyes, set in gleaming platinum the color of hers.

"Just wanted you to remember I've got my eye on you."

The little groan that escaped her was partly from his joke and partly from the pleasure being ignited by his light nibbling kisses tracing her shoulder and the arm she was holding out.

"You certainly found the rings quickly, considering how early we left for Reno the morning I got out of the hospital."

"Quickly? I spent the full day after I took you down in the mine finding what I thought was right for you."

"You had an engagement ring for me all that time?"

"When you sat there with me in the dark of the

mine I knew you were part of my life. I was in love with you. I had to keep you with me. I intended to ask you to marry me when we were in Yosemite, but I kept waiting for the right time and place. What with bears and one thing and another, I never found the right moment."

"And when I came here to the trailer for dinner?"

"Lesson number one in being a loving wife: Never remind your husband of his mistakes, and that night was a lulu." Bret ended the admission with a kiss that set the water bed into seductive gentle waves of motion, causing D'oro's lightly floating body to follow and respond to every movement of his.

Slowly his mouth and his gentle hands began the loving, skillful excitement of every fiber of her body. She was glad they had plenty of time.

Enter a uniquely exciting
new world with

Harlequin
American Romance
^{T.M.}

Harlequin American Romances are the first romances to explore today's love relationships. These compelling novels reach into the hearts and minds of women across America... probing the most intimate moments of romance, love and desire.

You'll follow romantic heroines and irresistible men as they boldly face confusing choices. Career first, love later? Love without marriage? Long-distance relationships? All the experiences that make love real are captured in the tender, loving pages of **Harlequin American Romances**.

What makes American women so different when it comes to love? Find out with **Harlequin American Romance!**

Send for your introductory FREE book now!

Get this book FREE!

Harlequin American Romance

Twice in a Lifetime
REBECCA FLANDERS

Mail to:

Harlequin Reader Service

In the U.S.
2504 West Southern Avenue
Tempe, AZ 85282

In Canada
649 Ontario Street
Stratford, Ontario N5A 6W2

YES! I want to be one of the first to discover

Harlequin American Romance. Send me FREE and without obligation *Twice in a Lifetime*. If you do not hear from me after I have examined my FREE book, please send me the 4 new **Harlequin American Romances** each month as soon as they come off the presses. I understand that I will be billed only $2.25 for each book (total $9.00). There are no shipping or handling charges. There is no minimum number of books that I have to purchase. In fact, I may cancel this arrangement at any time. *Twice in a Lifetime* is mine to keep as a FREE gift, even if I do not buy any additional books.

Name _____ (please print)

Address _____ Apt. no. _____

City _____ State/Prov. _____ Zip/Postal Code _____

Signature (If under 18, parent or guardian must sign.)

154-BPA-NAPP

AR-SUB-200

CHARLOTTE LAMB

The outstanding author of more than 50 bestselling romances with her exciting new blockbuster...

a Violation

A dramatic contemporary novel for every woman who has feared to love!

Clare Forrester had everything life had to offer. Then fate intervened with a nightmare – a violent rape that changed traumatically Clare's existence and that of everyone close to her. And now, the question was, would the power of love heal the deepest wound a woman can know....